death

is not an option

death
is not an option

⚬ stories ⚬

suzanne
rivecca

W. W. NORTON & COMPANY

New York | London

Copyright © 2010 by Suzanne Rivecca

For information about permission to reproduce selections from this book,
write to Permissions, W. W. Norton & Company, Inc.,
500 Fifth Avenue, New York, NY 10110

For information about special discounts for bulk purchases, please contact
W. W. Norton Special Sales at specialsales@wwnorton.com or 800-233-4830

Manufacturing by Courier Westford
Book design by Joanne Metsch
Production manager: Julia Druskin

Library of Congress Cataloging-in-Publication Data

Rivecca, Suzanne.
Death is not an option : stories / Suzanne Rivecca. — 1st ed.
p. cm.
ISBN 978-0-393-07256-3 (hardcover)
I. Title.
PS3618.I8425D43 2010
813'.6—dc22

2010011904

W. W. Norton & Company, Inc.
500 Fifth Avenue, New York, N.Y. 10110
www.wwnorton.com

W. W. Norton & Company Ltd.
Castle House, 75/76 Wells Street, London W1T 3QT

1 2 3 4 5 6 7 8 9 0

For Tatiana,

Panthera tigris altaica,

2003–2007.

contents

acknowledgments

The Wallace Stegner Fellowship in Creative Writing at Stanford University afforded me the time and support to write many of these stories. I am thankful for the advice and feedback of Tobias Wolff, Eavan Boland, Valerie Miner, Steve Polansky, Patricia Clark, and Bill Osborn. I am grateful for the love and wisdom of my parents, James and Anne Rivecca, and my sister, Colleen Rivecca. They have contributed in different ways to the genesis and evolution of this book, as have the following friends, new and old: Rita Mae Reese, Cameron McHenry, Abigail Ulman, Alex Lemon, Josh Tyree, Emily Mitchell, Josh Weil, Carolyn McCormick, Mary Howe, Maggie Callahan, and Mary Patton. I am indebted to Elyse Cheney and Jill Bialosky for making the publication of this book possible; to the editors of the literary magazines where several of these stories were originally published; to the editors of the Pushcart Prize series and the *Best New American Voices* series; and to the National Endowment for the Arts, the MacDowell Colony, Bread Loaf Writers Conference, and Djerassi Resident Artists Program. I am also grateful to San Francisco's St. Anthony Foundation and Homeless Youth Alliance for opening my eyes to important truths I could not have learned on my own. Please look them up and donate. Their work saves lives.

Every day, in all possible ways, I am thankful for the miraculous Jim Gavin.

death

is not an option

death is not an option

I t's the first night of the retreat, the slide show is starting, and I pray to be spared from the *Free Willy* song, which the school administration geniuses have decreed the anthem of our senior year. And this is nothing new: every year they carefully pick *the* shittiest song they can find to "represent" Sacred Heart. Freshman year it was "U Can't Touch This." The year after it was "Whoomp! (There It Is)." License plates and bumper stickers were made up.

Each new attempt to convince us they're down with our jive talk is more horrific than the last. This is even worse than last year when Mr. Grealey brought in a rockin' hymn about how "ballistic" Jesus was and substituted it for the regular hymns in *Glory and Praise*, and every Mass we took Communion to the sounds of "Our God Is an Awesome God," which featured a drum machine and Whitesnake guitar solo. It made me wish I lived in the pre–Vatican II days when everything was in Latin and the nuns beat you with rulers.

Hold me like the River Jordan . . .

For a while I keep my mind off the horror by fondly recalling the time I devised a custom-made vocab self-test in preparation for the SATs. I created my *own* analogies. I did fill-in-the-blanks with tricky look-alike multiple-choice options like *ascetic* and *aesthetic.* Then I let it sit for a while before I took it, drinking strong tea and making obscene anagrams out of saints' names. That was fun, too. I got a 780 verbal. I got a scholarship to Brandeis, which will enable me to escape the acid-precipitating, mutant-amphibian-producing industrial wasteland of Muskegon. But I don't even care. I keep telling my parents, *Let me take it again! I'll get an 800 this time!* Not until the GREs roll around, prep guides thick as phone books, will I once again enter the glorious realm of vocab-memorization.

Kyra leans close in the dark and hisses, "Does this song actually have a name? Or is it referred to only as 'Free Willy'?"

"I don't know," I say. "But it makes me hate whales. It makes me want to go harpoon one."

"How come there are no pictures of *us* in this slide show?" Kyra says. She runs a hand through her glinty blond hair and a whiff of fake-papaya mousse hits me. "Are we not worthy of *Free Willy?*"

She's right. We—Kyra and me, Sasha and Gretchen—were forced to pose for cheesy pictures six months ago on Spirit Day for the purpose of later seeing ourselves in this slide show at the end-of-the-year weekend retreat at St. Monica's Cabins. The slide show is apparently so peerless in its majesty that they couldn't even wait for us to unpack before forcing us to view it. We got off the bus from Muskegon and were immediately herded to the main lodge through all this blue-green undergrowth riddled with Lyme-disease-carrying ticks, dragging all our shit after us, because the Sacred Heart Showcase just couldn't wait. And it's not like we flipped off the camera. We are too refined for that. We are pissed and we hate Sacred Heart, but we *are* refined. But we didn't smile either. Gretchen had her I'm-too-sexy-for-my-shirt look going, the horizon-gazing supermodel pout. The rest of us just slouched like disaffected youth. Which is probably why none of our pictures made it into this touching retrospective, despite the fact that we are the sole members of the student body who are literate and unlikely to get knocked up in a trailer or convicted of date rape by graduation.

I start getting a weird feeling during the umpteen stills from last semester's Festival of Faith "talent" show featuring Amber Golin's interpretive dance—streamers and a leotard were involved—to R.E.M.'s "Losing My Religion." She ruined that song for me forever, not to mention she completely missed the point—it's called "*Losing* My Religion," not "*Celebrating* My Patriarchal Religion with a Cheesy Streamer Dance Featuring My Huge Camel Toe." But Mr. Grealey, the "creative director" of the whole travesty, ate Amber's performance up because it contained the word *religion*.

I crane my head to peer down the aisle at Mr. Grealey, roosting there like an overgrown and demented Chucky doll with his fat pasty face and wildly curly red hair. I really try to get a good look, because the mere sight of him pisses me off royally and being pissed gives me the firm resolve I need to take myself in hand and stop tearing up like an asshole. Last semester I flunked his final exam because it consisted solely of the question, "What would you do if you were driving along and you stopped to assist a woman who was hitchhiking and she wanted you to drop her off at an abortion clinic where she was planning to terminate the life of her unborn child?" I wrote that I'd drop her off at the fucking clinic. I threw in some N.O.W. rhetoric. I got to use all these nonapplicable-to-daily-situations phrases I *never* get to use, like "inchoate masses of noncognizant tissue"—which triggered a red-inked frowny face in the margin—and "violation of bodily integrity." I referred to the uterus as an "impregnable fortress" and chuckled happily at my ironic wordplay. Mr. Grealey not only gave me an F for "moral ambiguity," but accused me of "using an excessive amount of adjectives." Fuck me if I was going to let that screw my chances of going to college and getting the hell out of Muskegon, so I got my dad involved—he talks and talks and talks until people capitulate just to shut him up—and the School Board decided I could take a "make-up" exam, which consisted of identifying quotes from the New Testament. You see, the Old Testament is for Jews.

In Fostering Faith, Mr. Grealey shared with us the fact that he and his wife practiced the withdrawal method of contraception because it didn't violate the rules of the Pope. For months Kyra and Sasha and I verbally painted graphic scenes of Mr. Grealey pulling out in the height of passion and writing *Jesus Saves* on the wall with his spurting seed. We were completely grossing each other out but we kept talking about it, which is just as fucked-up, I guess, as Mr. Grealey himself disclosing such a thing to a roomful of seventeen-year-olds.

Free Willy ends. Now it's that Enigma song with monks chanting to some house music techno beat. What is the *point*? Why is this school obsessed with Jesus-songs set to drum machines?

"What kind of monks sing to house music?" I ask Kyra.

She says, "You know, the gay monks who like to go clubbing."

"It's a special religious order," I say. "Like the Franciscan monks. The Fran-sissies, if you will."

"I will not," she says coolly. We love that. The "if you will"/"I will not" combo. We are cracking up as pictures of the Senior Fall Picnic flash by.

"Oh, it never gets old," I say.

Finally it's the final slide: a close-up of the sooty red brick façade of Sacred Heart with its fake Pietà in front. The lights come on. And Mr. Grealey—whom the Mental Giants, under the delusion that they're black, refer to as "G-Man"—ascends the stage to staggered shouts of his nickname. "Here we go," he says. "The moment we've been waiting for: the official results of the Class of 1994 Mock Election! Drumroll, please."

Kyra kicks me in the shin. Then she lolls her head on my shoulder as Amber Golin is deemed "most creative." Scott Branson, king of the Mental Giants, is voted "most athletic." Gretchen is "quietest." When this one is announced, Claire McCready, who has lately appointed herself my cross-clique ambassador, leans forward at the end of the row and gives me a big toothy grin.

I give her a big dorky thumbs-up even though I couldn't give less of a shit.

I met Claire back in ninth grade, when I was new to Sacred Heart. We live eight blocks apart so we hung out, but she was a sadistic psycho bitch. She'd sneak up behind me with a stapler and staple a big hunk of my hair. Or take off her nasty sweaty loafer and shove it in my face, forcing me to smell it. She'd say, "Your hair is so weird, it's like *black* people's hair," and "You walk like a *cowboy*." When I started making friends with Kyra and Sasha and Gretchen she announced, "I'm moving up in the world," and promptly befriended the Mental Giants and Amber Golin.

Eventually, though, I became Claire's pet. The first day of junior year in the middle of the cafeteria line she said, "You know, you are so hilarious." Then she announced, "I thought Emma was the most boring person on earth when I first met her, but oh my God, she is *so* funny." And her friends all stared like they expected me to do a fucking pratfall.

So when the Mock Election categories were revealed, Claire kicked off her mission. "Kristi told me she was putting you down for 'quietest,'" she informed me, "and I'm like, 'She is *so* not quiet. She's hilarious!' And Kristi said, 'Well, she never talks to me.' And I'm like, 'Well, maybe that's because you're a fucking bitch.' Anyway, don't worry, it won't be you."

It is a mixed victory because I can only assume Claire's influence was responsible for Gretchen taking the title instead of me, and this is the kind of thing that really embarrasses Gretchen. She blushes beet-red on a dime. Despite that, she is technically *less* quiet than me. She can give a presentation in class without shaking and sweating and having a coronary. She never blurts out ridiculous non sequiturs when addressed by a Mental Giant. She is not besieged by senseless crying fits. She

has a little patron, too: Amber Golin, who is on a crusade to
force Gretchen to go to the prom. "*All* the guys think you're
really pretty," she told her earnestly one day in the cafeteria.
"You just need to be more outgoing!" Indeed, Gretchen's
only real qualification for the title is her blushing.

I peer down the aisle. Gretchen's face is so red it's almost
glowing. I roll my eyes at her. She stares at the floor.

Then Kyra wins "best eyes." Her eyes are blue and I guess
they're nice eyes. When Mr. Grealey announces her name, she
turns to me with an unreadable expression and I reach out a
finger and smooth her eyebrows, which although sparse and
blond are perpetually disheveled. She puts her head on my
shoulder again.

"Old Shep," I say, and pet her head.

We are finally allowed to retire to our sleeping quarters: a little
shantytown of rickety-ass cabins crammed on the edge of a
gravel trail. Each member of the Sacred Heart Class of 1994
appears to have the same Sears, Roebuck brand of rolling suitcase and we drag them in unison, an unbroken growl of dozens of tiny wheels on gravel for what feels like about ten miles.
Free Willy is stuck in my head. I stay close to Gretchen and
Kyra and Sasha. I've never been to the Upper Peninsula
before—the Sacred Heart bus had to traverse a treacherous,
swaying bridge over some Great Lake to get here—and this
landscape is not helping my imminent freak-out. The trees are
all fascist-looking and crowded together regimentally, in
gauntlets. I have caught wind of the phrase "mandatory canoe
trip." There are vicious rumors of a swimming hole. I feel my
heart tightening and I think for the millionth time that I prob-

ably have pleurisy—which the SAT prep guide defined as *an
inflammation of the thin layers of tissue (pleura) covering the lungs
and the chest cavity*—and I trudge along, staring at the triangular
Guess label on the laboring butts of Amber Golin and Claire,
who are accustomed to rustic woodsy jaunts like these from
their many consecutive years of posh summer camp. They
drag their suitcases with an air of weary entitlement, breaking
branches off trees and waving them around idly. They look like
they expect the trees to miraculously animate and go fetch them
a mint julep. Others, like Scott Branson, who are sent to Sacred
Heart for old-fashioned Catholic reasons, not college-prep reasons, seem unsure of what to do with the allotted pastoral leisure time. Smack in the middle of the herd is the contingent
represented by Kyra, Gretchen, Sasha, and me, whose parents
have nondescript jobs that produce enough income to send us
to Sacred Heart without having to hit up the congregation for
tuition assistance. But we're not getting cars for graduation.

My dad works at Butterworth Hospital and he's not a doctor but it's unclear what exactly he does. I have no clue what
Kyra's dad does besides the fact that he sings in some weird
Catholic men's chorus. Sasha's mom teaches community-
college English. Gretchen's parents are farmers. She is the only
one of us who looks at ease in all this flora and fauna. Halfway
to the sleeping cabins, a rabbit with a cotton-tail bounces across
our path and stands inches away staring at us boldly, and we all
ooh and ahh at it but Gretchen just yawns and says, "It probably has rabies. Or else it wouldn't come so close to us." She
and Sasha wander ahead. Kyra and I follow.

As we're walking, Josh Bowers catches up to us. He's like
Indonesian or something, but with eerily translucent and rosy

cheeks. He was adopted by blond do-gooders who would be perfect WASPs if they weren't Catholic.

"Emma," he says to me, "what are you doing when school's over?"

"I don't know," I say. I drag my suitcase with enhanced vigor.

"You don't *know*?" he says.

"Nope," I say.

"So you're not doing *anything*?" Josh Bowers says. "*I'm* going to the Citadel."

"Oh my God," I blurt out in horror. Then, more calmly, I say, "Oh."

We keep walking. He senses our conversation has reached its peak and he drifts off. Kyra says to me, "What the hell was *that*?"

"I *know*," I say. I think she's talking about the absurdity of Josh Bowers going out of his way to confide his misogynistic post-high-school plans.

"Why'd you say you're not doing anything?" she says. Then she pretends to be me, talking like Scarlett O'Hara: "Oh, I'm gettin' married right out of high school, none of that book-learnin' for me!"

Whenever I say something stupid Kyra finds it necessary to mimic me in a Southern accent. Neither of us has ever been farther south than Indiana.

"Well, what do you want me to do, pull out the résumé?" I say. "I don't want to have a big heart-to-heart with that ass-hole."

"College, what's *that*?" She is still doing the accent. "I'm stayin' on the plantation!"

Kyra knows that I'm going to Brandeis, which I chose because it's in New England and the campus is predominantly Jewish and there are no Catholics running around, but I try to avoid the subject because it is one of the many topics of conversation that triggers uncontrollable crying jags lately. It's ridiculous. I am not a crier. I never *have* been a crier. I've been daydreaming for years about escaping this hellhole and being surrounded by liberal and scholarly Zionists. And yet whenever college is mentioned, especially in a we're-so-proud-of-you or we'll-miss-you tone, I start sobbing. And not in a bittersweet, coming-of-age, I'm-at-a-crossroads way. In a major, pathological, impending-doom way. Now that the end of my cohabitation with them is in sight, my parents have been extra-sweet. They don't even yell at me anymore about being antisocial and having no extracurricular activities. It makes me feel even worse, like I'm an ungrateful little bitch who's abandoning them for the Jews. It makes me wish I had the kind of parents who beat me with a belt, like on a TV movie-of-the-week I saw called *Mommy, That Hurts*. I'd beat *myself* with a belt, if I thought it would snap me out of this.

The cabins are wood-paneled, with maroon carpet that smells like the evergreen-shaped things you hang from dashboards. Each room has two bunk beds. Next door to us is a group of girls that everyone makes fun of, including one who wears too much glittery silver eye shadow and this weird diabetic girl, Melody, who's always talking about giving herself insulin shots in the ass.

"Hey," she shouts out at Kyra and me as we enter, "want to watch me drop my drawers?" She's got this big needle in her hand.

"No," Kyra says. We close the door.

Gretchen and Sasha are unpacking. There's a big crucifix on the wall. Claire McCready wanders in. "Emma!" she says. Then she gives me a big sloppy kiss on the cheek and rumples my hair. She gets in these giddy effusive moods where she treats me like I'm some adorably crotchety old man, like Daddy Warbucks, and she's the irrepressible urchin trying to loosen me up. I shrug her off. "You are so damn cute!" she says.

"I'm not sleeping on top," Sasha says. "I'm a restless sleeper. I don't want to roll off and break my neck."

"Fine," I say. She's often bitchy when thrust into unfamiliar locales. I toss my bag upward, aiming for the top bunk, but it falls short and ends up whacking me on the head on the way down. Predictably, my eyes fill with tears. The room erupts in laughter.

"You're such a queer," Kyra says tolerantly.

Rubbing my head, I say, "What does a bag falling on my head have to do with my sexual orientation?"

No one has an answer to my question so I flop down on Kyra's bed, still rubbing my head, and start fondling her portable alarm clock. Everyone talks about how queer I am for a couple more minutes and then the conversation segues into a rousing game of Death Is Not an Option.

Claire says, "You have to have sex with either Mr. Grealey or Mrs. Bryce." Mrs. Bryce is the school librarian.

A consensus is reached that Mrs. Bryce would be preferable, because Mr. Grealey could impregnate you with his demon spawn.

"No, he couldn't," Sasha says. "He pulls out, remember?"

Laughter ensues. I turn over on my stomach and wish I could just be alone.

The next proposition is Gretchen's. "You have to drink a cup of piss or a cup of menstrual blood."

"Piss," Claire says immediately. "I'm not drinking *blood*."

"What if it was just regular blood, not menstrual blood?" Gretchen says.

I pipe up, "Menstrual blood hardly has any blood in it anyway. It's mostly uterine tissue. The blood just makes everything else red."

I do not know what comes over me.

"Oh, okay," Sasha says. "That settles it. We've got the vaginal-secretion expert over here."

I look at her and it occurs to me that I hate the pale-pink lip gloss she's been wearing for the past four years and the fact that she has no chin.

"Do you save it, Emma?" Claire asks. Her voice is high and sweet. "Is that your extra credit project for biology?"

They all laugh.

I put my face in Kyra's pillow. They've hit a sore spot, because I *do*, in fact, have an absurd and disgusting fixation with my own crotch. No one suspects the depths of my depravity. Technically, it's the Mental Giants' fault, because they always made jokes about women's pussies—in their vernacular—smelling like fish, and I wanted to know if it was true. I never noticed a fishlike smell on myself, but I figured perhaps the fishiness was located in some secret crypt I hadn't discovered yet. And this slime was gushing out of me on a regular basis—which is normal, according to the gyno guidebook I stole from my mom—so one day I decided to smell it.

I was cringing the whole time with perverse and sick fascina-
tion but I lifted up this big blob that was stuck to my underwear and I knew from its low level of viscosity—*comparable
to methanol*, said the gyno book, with *minimum resistance to
pouring*—that this was the *hospitable* kind of mucus, the ovula-
tory kind that grabs sperm and ushers them through to the
finish line, and it seemed so bizarre to see it hanging out in the
open air like something expendable and eliminative. I could
sense its willful and blindly grasping nature, its procreative
potential. It formed a tight clasping hood over my finger. It
seemed alive, like an amoeba. And it didn't smell fishy at all.

So this kicked off a secretion-obsessed fetish. It's sick. I'm
obsessed with what is pouring out of my crotch, despite my
monthly dread of my period due to the fact that I cannot figure out how to use a tampon. And, to compound the trauma,
the first time I tried was in front of *Claire* of all people, in her
bathroom, when I was fifteen and we were supposed to go
swimming in the bayou. I hate swimming and anyway the
Muskegon bayou is more liquid shit than water, but Claire
couldn't risk the public beach because someone important
might see her there with me. So she gave me this box of tam-
pons and I ended up staying in there for forty-five minutes. I
took a hand mirror and searched for my vagina. I'd been surprised by all the bulge and clutter; I had pictured something
like a vacuum hose, so I thought, well, maybe I don't *have* a
vagina. The diagrams provided by the tampon manufacturers
depicted it as symmetrical, dark-pink, and oval. Angle the
tampon toward your lower back, the instructions said. Rotate
the applicator while pushing, if you encounter resistance.

I read the dry authoritative reasonableness of those instruc-

tions with their pink print and felt a little-kid despair, a sink-
ing, whiny exhaustion, *You say it'll be easy but it's not really,* and
just the fact that there was a standardized, illustrated *procedure*
for something so personal and obscene made me feel as if I'd
been given complicated equipment that was wasted on me.
My vagina snarled itself into a little twisted bunch of closed-off
flesh, like a navel, and after a while Claire was pounding on
the door and saying, "What are you *doing*?" and I felt like I was
trying to perform surgery with a Tinkertoy.

Claire would not shut up about it for two weeks. I know
she told her friends. And I still cannot do it, despite the deep
and personal relationship I now have with my crotch.

By the time my head emerges from the pillow they're on a
new topic. Claire wants to know all about some date Gretchen
had six months ago with a guy she works with at Meijer
Grocery.

"Why won't you *say* anything?" Claire says. She's got the
wheedling Orphan Annie tone going.

"I'm not talking about it," Gretchen says.

"Did he kiss you?" Sasha drawls. She's rubbing lotion on
her pink freckled hairless legs.

"Will you get *over* it?" Gretchen's turning red.

"Oh my God, Gretchen!" Claire says. Her voice gets low
and quivery. "Did he *rape* you?" Then she bursts out
laughing.

"No!" Gretchen's bright red now. "God, his *mom* was on
the fucking date with us."

"Ooh," Claire says. "A threesome!"

This causes more hilarity. Claire and Sasha keep badgering
Gretchen, but she pulls the gray-wool camp blanket over her

head. Claire asks if the mom was wearing a strap-on. Sasha doubles over.

"You guys are dis*gust*ing," Gretchen wails from under the blanket. "You really want to hear sex details, ask Kyra. She's the big ho."

Kyra, the only one of us with a boyfriend, shrugs. Her boyfriend Jeff goes to the public school and approves of none of us. He thinks Sasha is too anal-retentive, Gretchen is too whiny, and I am a lesbian.

Sasha says, "You and Jeff are having sex?"

Kyra nods, wide-eyed, like it was a stupid question. I gasp and look over at Sasha, who just drawls, "What a whore."

Kyra ignores her. She's looking at me. She says, "Claire and Gretchen know."

"*Claire* knows?" I can't disguise the outrage in my voice. "Why don't *I* know?"

"Because I knew you'd freak out," Kyra says coolly. "Miss I-Hate-Men."

She's right, I suppose, because my mouth is still hanging open. I blurt out, "I thought you were on the pill for *cramps*!"

They find this hilarious.

I keep staring. I cannot believe she's having sex and didn't tell me. She shows me all the sappy notes she writes to Jeff and lets me correct their grammar. She calls me every week after *90210* so we can mock the shitty dialogue. She *knows* I hate Claire.

I think of my solitary and frequent masturbation sessions, my crotch explorations, and I cringe.

Now Claire is in comforting mode. "Oh, it's not a big deal," she says. "God, Emma, you know how you are about guys.

You're always like, 'He's an asshole, *He's* an asshole.' You hate all the guys in our class."

"That's because all the guys in our class are assholes," I say. It is an autopilot response, because I am still in shock. Sasha and Kyra groan, readying themselves for my oft-heard recitation of reasons *why* every guy in our class is an asshole. I will not grace them with it; but I *do* hate every guy in our class, and I cannot understand why they don't. There are two types of males at Sacred Heart and, depending on the economic situation of their parents, they will grow up to either pass conservative legislation or pump gas. Either way, they will be potbellied and balding. Some of them are *already* getting fat.

The first variety is the Mental Giant, e.g., Scott Branson, who spent the first two months of our Freshman Faith seminar looming over me and saying, "Are you scared of me? What do you think I'm going to do to you? Do you think I'm going to rape you? Maybe I will, maybe I will rape you."

One day some girl said, "*God*, Scott. Leave her alone. Can't you see she's scared?"

"Oh, like I'm serious," Scott Branson said. "Like I'd rape *her.*"

The second species is the Rush Limbaugh disciple, of which Josh Bowers is a prototype. The Limbaugh disciples watch that idiot's show and some of them even carry his book around like a Bible. They don't threaten to rape me and they occasionally talk to me like I am an actual human being and joke with me in the hallways, but this does not change the fact that the Rush Limbaugh disciples are assholes as well.

"Emma," Kyra says now, leaning on one elbow, "you're

just so weird about guys. Don't you ever just get a crush on anyone?"

And I know this is supposed to be the time of life when romantic shit occurs, but I'm not lowering my standards and going after some dickhead just so I can have a fucking pressed gardenia in a scrapbook to look back on in my elderly years and fondly recall how said dickhead forced himself on me in a backseat. I mean, I've read *Against Our Will*. I keep informed of all the atrocities men commit due to their hideous hormonal makeup and whatever other biological or social factors compel them to insert their appendages, unsolicited, into an opening that, in my case, can't even accommodate a light-flow Junior Miss tampon. The only male I've ever had a crush on is Eddie Vedder, because I saw that episode of *MTV Unplugged* when he wrote *Pro-Choice* on his arm with a marker. Sometimes Claire and I sit in her room and gush over Eddie Vedder and talk sadly about his traumatic childhood, for Claire is in love with him, too, though not for the pure and ideological reasons that I am. She just thinks he's hot. Claire is the only one who knows about my Eddie Vedder thing because, although she is a psychotic bitch, a hokey part of me is reserved for her, a part I can get out of my system and feel better. Claire is kind of like an enema.

Now Claire says, "Emma *does* have a crush on somebody." She looks around solemnly.

"Shut up, Claire," I say.

"Emma is obsessed with Eddie Vedder," Claire announces.

"That guy from Pearl Jam?" Sasha shoots me an accusatory look. "Didn't he like kill himself last month?"

"No," Gretchen says. "That was Kurt Cobain."

"You like *him*?" Kyra giggles. She sticks one leg in the air and her sweatpants ride up. She scratches her leg. I think, *That is the leg of a person who is sexually active.* Then she starts singing "Jeremy" in a guttural baritone. "Does that song get you hot, Emma?"

"Claire," I say, "I hate you." She can tell I mean it. I know she's going to corner me later and try to have some big heart-to-heart and tousle my hair and tell me I'm cute, and I will tell her I am not her fucking bad-tempered sugar daddy.

Afterward, following dinner in the main lodge and Mass in a musty barnlike chapel—during which I shook no one's hand at the *peace be with you* part—I can't sleep. My pleurisy kicks in and I feel like there's a starfish flexing in my chest. Tomorrow night this fucking retreat will be over. In a month and a half I will graduate. In four months I will go to college. I used to comfort myself with that thought, like a nest egg. But now I feel the crying jag starting. I have been here too long; I have grown conditioned; I only know how to interact with human beings who are in direct and antagonistic opposition to me.

I pound my head softly on the pillow.

In movies, the thoughtful outcast girl always has some sort of nonschool lifeline, some *outlet* that affirms her faith in humanity, for instance a supportive gay guy, or a nice old person who passes on wisdom. I have nothing. I'm not even good with adults—I'm too nervous and shifty-eyed and bitter—and old people hate me. I know this for a fact. We had to do forty hours of community service in order to graduate, and I did it at Everest Nursing Home, where almost every resident was demented or extremely crotchety. Or just depressing. There was this one lady who sat in her bed all day watching figure-skating footage of Nancy Kerrigan, over and over and over. She just stared at it listlessly. It made me want to die.

I try to match my breathing to Sasha's, in the bunk below me, and after a while it works and I sleep. But then I have a weird dream that my dad is John Lennon, or at least that I'm raised to *believe* he's John Lennon. But he still goes to work every day at Butterworth Hospital. Eventually I realize that John Lennon not only looks nothing like my dad but is British and also dead, and my mom admits that my dad is delusional but we should just humor him. So he's sitting around in his suit and bifocals and saying, *Ah, yes that last concert in Candlestick Park was a heady time indeed,* and I'm like, *Dad, tell me about when you had that bed-in for peace!* When I wake up I'm shaking. It's still night. I'm feeling really sad and wanting to talk to my dad on the phone.

But I don't know where there *is* a phone. We are trapped here with no modern conveniences. And it's like four in the morning. So I get out of bed as quietly as I can and grope my way down the hall to the door, which, to my surprise, is unlocked.

Outside, the darkness feels like something touchable pressing against me, like those rough black strips that cover the windshield in car washes. There's a smell of fir and smoke. I just keep slogging through tall damp grass with no idea where I'm going, and after a while it occurs to me that I am humming the *Free Willy* song. I punch myself in the stomach. It doesn't feel like anything so I do it again, but then it hurts, a lot, and I start crying. Snot is coming out of my nose and I cry, walking along, until my eyes start to adjust to the dark and I can make out the shapes of trees and clearings and other cabins.

The crying thing doesn't even faze me anymore. I'm growing accustomed to it, like a perpetual cough. I know I just
have to let it run its course and eventually the impending-
doom feeling will stop and I'll be okay for a while. But then a
goose flits by, or maybe a pheasant, reminding me of when I'd
walk home from grade school through the noxious birth-
defect-producing chemical miasma of Muskegon and I'd day-
dream about woods and wildlife and Pine-Sol-crisp air. I was
brainwashed by Laura Ingalls Wilder. And here I am in this
lovely natural setting and I'm so fucked that I can't even look
at a pheasant and think, *Wow, what a wondrous being.* All I can
do is criticize it. I think, *Nice feathers*.

This exacerbates the crying.

And to top it all off there's a rustling in the reeds about a
yard away—what is this, *Wind in the Willows?*—but it's not
another woodland creature. It's a person, and the gait is unmistakably male.

I freeze and stand in a tall clump of some sort of beach grass,
waiting for the figure to pass. But I can tell he sees me. He's
coming toward me, and he's pushing vegetation out of the
way like Conan the Barbarian, and I see the tautness of his
neck and the blindly glandular glint in his eye and the purposeful balling of his fists, and I think, *Well, this is it, I am
fucked. Whoever this is will probably rape me.* And every fear and
joy of my life narrows to a terrible and piercing culmination. I
curse myself for weighing ninety-eight pounds and actually
being *proud* of that fact, I curse myself for not paying attention
to the self-defense guy who visited tenth-grade gym class and
showed us how to wrench someone's wrist.

"Who is that?" a male voice says. Slightly high, smooth,

tempered with self-conscious suavity. The voice of Josh Bowers, future Citadel cadet. "Who is that?" he says again. And I start crying again, with anger this time, with the helpless draining of all that fizzy adrenaline, the fear less painful than the senseless reprieve: Josh Bowers, whole and confused and harmless, walking out of the bushes.

"Hey," he says one more time. "Who *is* that?"

And I cannot say my name. I cannot stand to see the disappointment or derision that will dawn on Josh Bowers's face when he finds out I am not Amber Golin, or Claire, or even Gretchen, that I am Emma Aleramo and I am having a fucking crying fit in the middle of the woods at four a.m.

"Is that Emma?" Josh Bowers says. Then he comes closer. I can see his abnormally rosy cheeks. He smells like shaving cream, which strikes me as ridiculous considering his apparent lack of facial hair follicles or pores. His skin is better than mine. "Emma, are you *crying*?"

"No," I say. I cross my arms and take a couple steps back from him. "I'm going for a walk. I can't sleep."

"Oh my God," he says. "You're *crying*." He says it in this full-of-childish-awe voice.

"No, I'm not," I say.

"You don't have to *deny* it," he says. "It's a natural human function. Human beings have emotions."

"Oh, fuck off," I say. That doesn't feel as cathartic as I thought it would. I wipe my nose fiercely.

"Do you want to talk about it?" he says. But I remember how he's a member of the Students Helping Students counseling brigade—as is Claire—and I refuse to be his fucking case study.

"No," I say.

Josh Bowers sits down on a convenient log. He's wearing his customary Dockers and rugby shirt, and I feel underclothed in my pajamas.

"I couldn't sleep, either," he says. He takes a pack of cigarettes out of his pocket and fishes a lighter out. The way his wrists and hands undulate as he does this, and their delicate veins, is attractive. I hate that. He says, "Want one?"

"No," I say. Then I point and laugh. The impending-doom sensation ebbs. "Are those Virginia Slims?"

He shrugs. "Yeah, laugh it up. They're my mom's, okay?" He exhales smoke.

"You've come a long way, baby," I say.

To my surprise, he laughs loud. I sit down on the opposite end of the log. It's wet.

"I feel like we're in a living room," he says. "Like this isn't even the real woods. Like they just took this log and plunked it down in the middle of like a stage set." Smoke trails out of his mouth.

I don't know what to say to that.

Then he says, "So are you really not doing anything after school? Are you going to be a hermit and live in a cave?"

I say, "Are *you* really going to South Carolina to become a brainwashed android?"

It surprises me when he laughs again. "That's the plan," he says.

We sit for a while and chat haltingly about how much everything sucks. In the moonlight the hairs on his forearm look silvery and hypersensitive, like cat whiskers. For a second I feel sort of not-myself. Happy. Then I am pissed at myself for feeling happy just because some asshole is talking to me.

Then Josh Bowers says, "You *are* going to college, aren't you?"

I pick up a leaf. It's slimy and appears to be decomposing. "I'm going to Brandeis."

"Well, why are you all *embarrassed* about it?" he says. He inches forward and looks into my face. His eyes are wide. "Is that what you were crying about?"

I stand up, because I realize what he's doing to me. Joke with her. Laugh at her witticisms. Gently lead her to the crucial subject. Claire showed me the Students Helping Students training book with all its guided exercises. Josh Bowers is fucking *practicing* on me. I will become a test case for next month's Students Helping Students meeting, and Josh Bowers will be given some special badge.

I say, "I'm going back. 'Bye." And he's all in my face now with the Barbara Walters what-kind-of-tree-would-you-be look, and I am not falling for it.

"What?" he says. "What'd I say?" He throws his arms wide open.

The tears are coming again. "Fuck off," I say. It doesn't feel cathartic this time, either.

The following morning, no one comments on the fact that I've been wandering the woods weeping half the night like some fucking Brontë-sister lass. By ten, though, I am composed. As we're waiting in line for muffins in the main lodge, Amber Golin bounces along and asks of the entire world, "Isn't Gretchen so pretty?" She's turning her head around, looking for affirmation. Gretchen is bright red. "Doesn't she look like Winona Ryder?"

Kyra says, "I think she looks like Wynonna Judd." Gretchen giggles.

Amber says, "Oh my God. You guys are so *mean* to each other."

After breakfast, there is an idiotic collage-making exercise. I get stuck in a group with Scott Branson, Amber, and Brady O'Toole, a Limbaugh disciple.

"You have to add something here, Emma," Brady says. He gestures impatiently at the pile of chopped-up magazines that surround us. I cut out a picture of a sailboat. I cut very carefully, so that there are no white edges showing, and I glue it to the sheet of poster-board, right between Amber's fluffy white kitten and Scott's Detroit Lions quarterback.

"So what's the meaning of that?" Brady says.

I shrug. "You told me I had to add something. So I added something."

I stare down at the poster-board, and it looks as if the kitten is about to take an ominous sailboat journey to see the quarterback. It is an expedition out of which no good can come.

After the display of the collages, during which Brady O'Toole announces, "And this is Emma's great contribution," while scornfully indicating my sailboat, Mr. Grealey heaves his doughy body up from its cross-legged repose. He claps his hands.

"All right, people," he says. "I want everyone in a circle. I want a big circle right in the middle of the floor."

People start wearily dragging chairs.

"No!" Mr. Grealey intones, waving his short arms in protest. "On the floor! We're going to *sit* in a circle on the floor."

Suddenly Kyra is beside me. "No," she breathes in my ear. "Not a circle of love."

Her breath smells sweet and pink, like Carefree gum. I smile reflexively, but she drifts away. The starfish wakes up inside my chest. A cactus climbs up my throat.

Then a boom box is produced, and the *Free Willy* song soars across the rough-hewn rafters.

All around me, I am aware of people's heads lowering in staggered motion. They are dropping like flies. They swarm and dip around my peripheral vision. Then I notice I am taller than everyone else and it takes me a while to realize it's because I'm the only one still standing up. When I sink to the ground it feels like a swoon. I am uncomfortably conscious of my tail-bone. We, the Sacred Heart Class of '94, are in a raggedy circle. We are eyeing each other. For a moment it occurs to me that Mr. Grealey is about to orchestrate a gladiator cage match to the lush sounds of *Free Willy*, that this is what they have been training us for: a flesh-and-blood reenactment of the holy war fought by our school mascot, the Catholic Crusader, in which only the true believers will be weeded out and saved.

Then Mr. Grealey says, "We are going to go around this circle, and I want everyone to step into the middle and share what they'll miss most about Sacred Heart."

Not far from it.

Scott Branson is first. And Scott Branson is crying. Snuffling, actually, with those shoulder-heaving rip-snorting ram-in-heat spasms that pass for crying in Mental Giantland. He stamps his feet, as if about to charge. He chokes out, "I love you guys! If anyone ever needs anything, just ask and I'll deliver. I mean it." His sincerity is terrible. Mr. Grealey enters the circle and gives Scott a manly shoulder-clap. More Mental Giants follow. And they are all crying. It's horrifying.

Then it's a clump of Limbaughs, all in a row, one after the other delivering their smooth polished orations. Some are choked up. Josh Bowers says, "I always tried to be a good person. I mean, I'll *continue* to try to be a good person. I think . . . I think it's my destiny to help people." His eyes are wide and pliant and no one mocks him even though he is a pompous windbag who did not even follow Mr. Grealey's simple instructions.

And then there's Kyra. They like Kyra, they're calling for her—"Ky-RA, Ky-RA"—and she languidly slides into the middle and looks all shy and says meekly, "Okay, okay, I don't really know what to say but I don't want you all to beat me."

"We love you, Ky," Gretchen calls. She and Sasha and Claire have big transfixed grins on their faces. Their faces are flushed. They have all simultaneously crossed over to the land of those with outward feelings, soft and malleable and unashamed, pure and cushiony as marshmallow fluff. Maybe they have lived there all along. They are all believers, my sex-having friends who will grow up to enter the world and make productive lives for themselves, buffered against emotional impoverishment.

They will be normal. They will be healthy. And the *Free Willy* song, I realize, is on repeat.

I have this feeling that I cannot name. It's driving me crazy because I am the Crossword Queen, the Vocabulary Vigilante; nothing in the English language has ever eluded me and it is ridiculous, how I cannot remember what you call it when you know that no matter what you say, what you do, you're screwed.

There's a term for this state of mind. A small jeweled box of a word.

Claire is in the middle now. And she is not crying at all. She's talking with that voice of hers, each word a little frozen dewdrop, and it's all gibberish to me until she says:

"I know what *I'll* miss most. I am gonna miss my sweet little Emma, who better write to me when she's at her smarty-pants college because Emma, baby, *you* are the shit." And a big Claire-hurricane descends. She's hauling me to my feet. She's manhandling me. Her head smells like scalp and Finesse. And there's a tough, muscular streak under all this puppyish gamboling. I see it in her eyes as she looks straight into my face, her righteousness smooth and unbroken as silver plating. And then I know that whatever her politics, whatever shiksa diety she half-assedly believes in, *Claire* could hold her own at a place like Brandeis. She could never crumble from the inside out. And maybe it's that, or maybe it's the internal snapshot of me in college at some leather-topped desk, obediently writing letters to Claire McCready—as I know I will—that starts the crying.

Of course everyone thinks I'm touched. In a good way. Of course I even feel the concentrated beam of Mr. Grealey's approval. Of course they're all thinking, *At last, at last.* Claire's soft arms are around my rib cage and she's murmuring "It's okay, it's okay," and there's a smell of sharp fir from the world outside and no one suspects the truth: I am crying because I, like the clairvoyant Josh Bowers, can see my destiny.

I see terminal therapy. I see myself drowning in a sea of dark progressive heads just like my own, collapsing upon a beautifully manicured campus topiary like a soldier falling on his sword. I see a counselor with a poly-blend twinset and deep circles under her eyes, and I see myself going to her every day and talking about my fucking feelings and how I cannot thrive in any but utterly hostile circumstances, how I don't know who I am unless I'm fighting and what the hell should I do, go back to Muskegon to reclaim my identity? And I can hear the counselor's voice. It's as clear and crystalline as Claire's. It says, Yes, go back. Go back to Muskegon with the Jesus freaks and die a thousand deaths every day because that is the only cure for your incessant, debilitating, and constant sense of *futility*. And I hear myself shouting, *That's* the word.

yours will do nicely

All night long I kept sneaking looks at the smiley face stamped on the back of my hand, proud of being old enough to drink even though I'd been twenty-one for six months already. By midnight I was so drunk my whole body was warm and numb and I kept smiling at absolutely nothing. I couldn't even remember a time when smiling took effort. I even stopped worrying whether or not people would think Tom and I were together. I danced the wiggly-armed hippie dance with him unashamedly until my calves seized up and my torso felt spongy, the old wood floor of the bar bouncing under our feet, the room tilting like a capsizing ship. The band was called Hearts of Gold on Fire and it had a mumbly singer whose lyrics I couldn't hear under a mess of keyboards and drums and guitars and fiddles and tambourines. I'd never seen a band with so many members and I kept wondering if I was having double vision. It was winter break.

"I need to stop," I said to Tom. "I feel like I'm going to fall. And puke. Fall and puke."

But my voice was sucked away by the music and Tom didn't hear me. He kept turning around and around in circles like he was on ecstasy. I waited until his back was turned and made my way across the dance floor to the bar, where the tall blond guy I'd had my eye on all night was leaning. Then I ordered a beer even though I hated beer.

"Hi," I said to the blond guy.

"You all right?" the guy said.

I studied his face and tried to figure out if it belonged to someone I could have sex with.

"Why do you look so sad?" the guy said.

I could feel Tom watching me covetously from the dance floor. I ignored him and kept gazing up at the strange guy. He had an easygoing stoner's handsomeness, blond but not too blond, hair in a ponytail, long fingers, and a surfer's good-natured squint. His eyes were hazel. He looked like the kind of person who ate Clif bars. Which was fine.

"I'm not sad," I said. "This is just the way my face looks."

He wore a long-sleeved T-shirt with a wolf face and a moon drawn on it. I commented on the wolf, and he started talking about how he radio-tracked and tagged them at the University of Wisconsin as part of the biology/environmental studies program he was in. It was getting late. I saw Tom and my roommate, Rachel, looking at me and whispering from across the room. The band was taking a break.

I took a napkin from the bar and a pen out of my patchwork

corduroy purse. I wrote on the napkin and gave it to the wolf
guy.

"I'm going home," I said to him. "This is my address. If you
want, come over in a couple hours. I'll make you some tea."

He looked a little surprised, but took the napkin. "Okay,"
he said. "That's really nice of you."

I nodded. I could feel myself sobering up a little, and a
strong undertow of depression pulled at me.

"Well," I said to the guy, "I will hopefully see you fairly
soon."

On the car ride home, Rachel kept shaking her head.

"Katrina," she said, "did you ask that person to come over
and have sex with you?"

"I told him tea," I said.

"He could have a disease," she said. "He could be a rapist." She
sounded like she was checking both of these things off a list.

Tom piped up, "You have to tell me *everything*, as soon as
he leaves."

I sat and watched East Town flash by: all the neon and
brick-paved streets and the people walking and smoking alone.
"He's cute, right?" I kept saying. "You think he's cute, don't
you, Rachel?"

"He has gross hair," she said. Rachel has known me since
high school and we used to like the same kind of guy: clean-
cut and preppy. She never forgave my defection.

"Rachel," I burst out, "you've sown your wild oats. And
you have a boyfriend. You can talk."

"I've *sown my wild oats*?" She looked appalled. "What the
fuck is that? I'm dropping you off and going to Josh's. I am not
staying around to witness this."

"I'll stay if you want," Tom said. "In case he tries anything."

I said, "I want him to. That's the *point*."

But once I was alone in the apartment, I wasn't sure.

I brushed my hair and flossed my teeth. I couldn't stop ripping the cuticles off my thumbs. Finally I fell into Rachel's
parents' cast-off La-Z-Boy and picked up one of Rachel's
magazines and tried to get myself all horny by reading the sex
tips. One of them was, *Flick your tongue firmly across the length of
your man's perineum.* There was a picture of a muscle-bound
male model, naked with his hands in front of his crotch, and a
corresponding diagram indicating his erogenous zones. As I
read the accompanying text, it struck me that the success of all
those tips rested on the assumption that you had *open, clear communication* with your partner about his and your *past experiences,
boundaries, and hang-ups.* Trust, the article said, was essential.

I thought of the first time I ever had sex, which was with
my ex-boyfriend. I interrupted him midway through and asked
him how it felt to be inside of me.

"Huh?" he said, breathing hard.

"How does it feel?" I said. "What does it feel like in
there?"

I could tell he was searching for an answer that would please
me. "I don't know," he breathed, then kissed my face. "It's
great. It's like I can feel you all around me."

I lowered my sweaty forehead to his shoulder and a sound
came out, strangled and too weak for the feeling behind it, the
sound you make in a dream where you try to scream and can't.
I was jealous. I wanted to feel myself all around me.

I closed Rachel's magazine. I started half hoping the guy

wouldn't show up. I didn't remember all that clearly what he even looked like.

When the doorbell rang a couple hours later I went down and let him in, fully sober. He was, too; I could tell. He looked around nervously. We smiled at each other.

"Just so you know," I said, "I don't usually do things like this."

"Well," he said, "I don't really know what you're planning on, like, doing with me. But whatever's cool. I don't have an agenda."

I remembered, as I filled the kettle with water, that his name was Jason. I made tea and brought it into the living room. He was sitting on the couch with Rachel's cat on his lap.

"Awesome," he said, sipping. "No one's ever offered me tea when I came to their house. I *love* tea."

"I have a lot of tea," I said. "I'm kind of obsessed with tea. And it's all organic."

I sat down next to him. It was weird. There were times when I could smell people, and there were other times when I just involuntarily shut that capacity off and went completely immune, and everything seemed asexual and clean as blank paper. That's how I felt on the couch with Jason. I wondered if it was because I hadn't had sex in two years, if the celibacy had permanently numbed some crucial pheromone receptor.

I put music on to make things easier. We began talking. He told me about his ex-girlfriend. He spoke about her with a word-searching, dazed deference that told me he wasn't over her at all. I mentioned a detail about my ex-boyfriend, some tidbit about how he loved mountain-biking. He had broken up with me two years ago but I made it sound much more recent. I also made it sound like it had been mutual. But even as I modulated my voice to convey judicial evenhandedness I could still hear the ghost of my ex, speaking in a voice lower than usual and softer, telling me I was manipulative and capricious, and I remembered how taken aback I'd been, despite my grief, by his correct and unassuming use of the adjective. Big words were *my* province. It was like being shot with my own gun.

"He's a decent guy," I said. I'd taken his letters and drowned them in a bathtub so I could watch his endearments blur into illegibility, but he'd written in indelible ink.

Jason stuck out his foot in its white sock and rubbed it across the cat's belly as she writhed on the floor, purring and extending all four legs.

"I miss having pets," he said. "I have two dogs at my parents' place."

I said, "What are their names?"

He flushed a bit and stopped rubbing the cat. "Keep in mind," he said, not looking at me, "I was, like, six at the time I named them."

"Okay," I said.

He was silent for a second. He started laughing. "Oh, man," he said. "You have to tell me something embarrassing back, then."

"Okay," I said.

"Their names," he said, folding his arms, "are Happy and Sad."

I started laughing, too. For the first time, I deliberately touched him, flicking the back of my hand against his arm. "That's so weirdly existential," I said.

"I was a prodigy," Jason said. He spoke with a deadpan mock-gravity; I recognized it as my own. It was this—his aping of my tone, not snidely, but accommodatingly—that filled me with sudden tenderness, and shame.

"Now it's your turn," he said.

I got up. For a second I pondered telling him I hadn't had sex in two years.

"I can't think of anything," I said. "I've never done anything embarrassing in my life."

"That sounds like a pretty good life," he said.

"It is," I said. "It's great."

About an hour later we went into the bedroom. I tried to make it unceremonious.

"You can sleep in Rachel's room or with me in my bed," I said. "I just want to give you an option."

He paused for a moment. "I guess I'd rather sleep with you."

"Okay," I said, too quickly. "Hold on a second."

I lit some patchouli incense.

"Whoa," Jason said. "It's getting pretty hippie in here."

I wondered if he was making fun of me. "Well," I said. "Some people think patchouli smells bad, but I like it because it smells like earth and dirt, you know? It's, like, an earthy, *real* smell." Jason didn't answer, and I knew I'd said it wrong. That patchouli thing was something I heard my friend Teal say once, only she made it sound breezy, serene. I tried to think of something else to say, but I couldn't tell when it was appropriate to stop talking and to start behaving as though we were about to have sex. So I just turned off the light. We climbed onto the bed fully clothed, on top of the covers. The bed was a single, with wheels on it that screeched in protest if budged. My parents bought it for me when Rachel and I moved out of the dorms in sophomore year.

I turned on my stomach and Jason lay on his side. I kept waiting for him to touch me. He kept breathing. His breath got more and more measured and I gave him up for lost. Then I finally felt his hand, warm and exploratory and purposeful, rubbing my upper back, and it was as though I neatly put a large part of myself aside, like hanging a bulky coat in the closet. I got on top of him and kissed him. His hands moved down to the seat of my patchwork corduroy pants and snaked under my shirt to stroke my back. He eased us over and got on top of me. A rhythmic clanking noise accompanied his movements, and he paused to take a metal tin of Altoids out of the pocket of his cargo pants. "Sorry," he said. He set it on the floor.

We separated. Then we sat apart from one another in the dark and undressed silently, self-consciously, like children in a dormitory preparing for bed. I thought, *I don't know this person.* I would not presume to undress him, to remove his shirt when he might be cold without it, to unbutton his pants like a warped mother—would I fold them? or throw them aside in a fit of carnal abandon?—but beyond those restricted, homely ministrations was something else, something I was entitled to, a territory understood by instinctual contract to be jointly owned. We were going to have sex. I could not remember why.

I'd sort of forgotten what a penis felt like. But Jason's felt just like my ex's. I wondered if they all felt the same. And as the sex was happening, I kept telling myself, *Notice everything. Feel all the feelings.* But I couldn't. I did exactly what I was afraid I'd do: I let it all go by like passing scenery through a car window. Nothing stuck.

After a couple minutes Jason stopped and whispered, "I'm really sorry. But I have to pee."

"Oh," I said. "All right."

He got up and scurried naked down the hall. I lay there with sweat drying on my stomach, feeling like a huge Band-Aid had been ripped off the entire front of my body. He stayed gone for a pretty long time after the toilet flushed. And by the time he came back in, it was like I'd spent an interval in cold storage. I was chilled. I saw his body silhouetted in the doorway and knew how I must have looked, lying there waiting passively for the fucking to resume, and at that moment I almost hated him. And it was clear that I was going to have to pretend he was a prop, like the vibrator Tom gave me, sort of as a joke but sort of not, for my twenty-first birthday. I was going to have to go at it as if I were alone.

"I want to be on top," I said.

Jason seemed a little surprised, but climbed into bed, scooted back against the wall, and stretched out. I sprawled on top of him, reached back and put his penis inside me and started to move. We didn't kiss. He ran his hands over my back and it felt like he was doing it because he didn't know what else to do, and was afraid of provoking a reprimand. He softened inside me and slipped out.

"Fuck," he half whispered.

I jerked him with my hand until he was hard and put it back in. After about half a minute he lost it again. We stopped and kissed, me tinkering with him all the while, and tried a third time. It happened again.

I climbed off him and propped my head on my palm. I heard the cat crying for her breakfast. I wondered when Rachel would be back from her boyfriend's and whether I could get Jason out in time so she wouldn't say something snide to him.

We lay there in silence for a while. Then Jason said, "Sorry I can't perform."

He said that like we were people who knew each other well, sharing a joke together.

"Don't worry about it," I said.

"No," he said, "I know what you probably think. And it's not that. It's not that I don't want to."

I looked at him, startled. It never occurred to me that he didn't.

"Because I do want to," he said. "This is nice. It's not like the last time I was with someone."

"What was that like?" I said.

"This German girl," Jason said. "This exchange student, down in Wisconsin. This was right after me and Val broke up. I hooked up with this girl once. We were drunk. She wanted it to become something more, and I didn't. Then a month later she came over to my apartment. She was really upset. She asked me to make love to her. And I couldn't do it—I mean, I didn't want to—and I had to tell her no. It was terrible."

I usually hated it when men used the term "make love." It sounded so squishy and earnest, like some kind of craft project. But then Jason put his arms around me and finally I could feel him, his hands intelligently registering all my bones and my skin, his lips burrowed in the crook of my neck and shoulder, and it was ridiculous how this made me so instantly happy, so relieved I'd been granted something another girl had been denied. I imagined her German face stern and spare with deprivation, and wondered what she had done wrong, and what I had done right. I slid into that detached sated space of knowing someone wants me.

"You're," Jason murmured. Then he said something I couldn't hear.

He started stroking my forehead and then my hair. He raked his hand slowly through it, up and down, again and again, pausing to knead my scalp. I shut my eyes.

"I'm what?" I said. I really wanted to know.

But he didn't answer.

Rachel came home and swooped up her cat, cradling it like a baby.

"What happened, Luna?" she asked the cat. "Did Katrina have sex? Did she have hippie tantric sex?" The cat stared into her face and began to twist back and forth.

"You traumatized her," Rachel said to me. She smiled at me brightly, brilliantly—the kind of smile she always flashed to show she was kidding, even if she wasn't. I was familiar with it from high school, even though she never used it on me then. Tom called it the Passive-Aggressive Grin.

"We made her watch," I said.

Rachel stared at me for a few seconds. At first she was expressionless. Then she looked ready to burst out laughing. Finally she made a big show of turning on her heel and leaving the room, walking extra slowly, as if afraid of detonating.

Her mood didn't improve all night. When we met Tom at his place before going to dinner in East Town, the first thing

Rachel said to him was, "Tom, I'd like you to meet my friend Smurfette."

I was wearing a homemade blue patchwork dress. It had been a birthday gift from Teal, before she'd told me I was copying her lifestyle and I stopped returning her calls. Rachel hated Teal, for her blondness and humorless equanimity as much as for her hippieness. She called her Stoner Barbie.

Tom looked back and forth from Rachel to me. "Katrina looks beautiful," he said to Rachel reprovingly.

"Thank you, Tom," I said. I was conscious of how prim I sounded.

"Okay," Rachel said. "Joke. Sorry I insulted your lover girl."

Then everything went dead and still.

"*What?*" Tom said. He raised his hands up and stared, wild-eyed and red-faced, from Rachel to me. "*What?*" I couldn't bring myself to look at him. Even Rachel cast her gaze down.

After dinner, Tom dropped Rachel off at her boyfriend's and me at the apartment.

"You've known each other too long," he said, as I gathered my bag and coat. "That's why you hate each other so much."

"We don't hate each other," I said. I felt a bolt of guilt, remembering Rachel and me in high school, inseparable, taking NoDoz in the mornings and bouncing around the chemistry lab with beakers of acid. We reworded the hymns in *Glory and Praise*, substituting each other's names for the Lord's: *Rachel I adore thee, lay my life before thee, how I love thee . . .*

"But you've outgrown each other," Tom said.

"I don't know," I said.

"She doesn't understand you anymore," he continued.

I looked at Tom, at his nerdy-chic plastic glasses and vintage bowling shirt, and I tried to remember how we became friends in the first place. All I knew was that ever since we'd met in our Culture of Minorities class (in which everyone, including us and the instructor, was white), he had taken it upon himself to *make* me his friend. And then, before I knew it, he was. I suddenly wanted Rachel beside me very badly, in the way I used to want my mother beside me if I hurt myself on the playground, just the intimate bulk of her, my own tribe, my *family*.

"That was a really short dinner," he said. "I've had orgasms that were longer than that dinner." He slapped my thigh briskly.

"Thanks for the ride," I said. I clambered out of the cab of his truck, my long skirt catching as I dropped to the pavement, and went inside and turned on the TV. I was worried he would call as soon as he got home and ask me what my problem was. But a few minutes later, as I was nodding off in front of a PBS show about orca whales, Jason called.

"Hey," he said. "I was just watching this TV movie about domestic violence and the girl in it looked exactly like you. I got this feeling, like I had to call and make sure you weren't being beat up or something." He cleared his throat and laughed uncomfortably. "I mean, that's not why I'm calling you really. But."

"I'm learning about whales," I said. I started sweating; I could smell myself. I shut off the whales.

We talked for a while without ever mentioning the sex. He told me about the timber wolves in Wisconsin.

"There was this one I put the radio collar on myself," he said. "We had her in a foot trap and had to sedate her. She had snow-white fur—you hardly ever see that—and her eyes looked like Petoskey stones. That kind of gray, you know?"

I asked how big the wolves are.

"About as big as a German shepherd, except everything about them is just narrower, kind of. This one, we've been tracking her for a year. And last month we found out she walked all the way from Eau Claire to the Upper Peninsula. By herself. She broke away from the pack and just set off by herself for hundreds of miles."

He sounded exhilarated, almost proud of her. He told me how the collars sometimes emit a long, flatline signal of non-movement, indicating the wolf is free of the tracking device, or else dead.

"That's the signal no one wants to hear," Jason said. He sounded dutifully grave, as though this were something he'd been trained to say if called upon to explain his work to laypeople.

He was going back to Wisconsin in two days. Before hanging up he told me how great our conversation was and how it was the best conversation he'd had all break. I was a little surprised, since I felt like I'd been kind of dull. But I was glad he didn't think so.

"We should write to each other," he said. "I called you first, so you should write me first."

"Okay," I said.

"Are you really going to?" Jason said. I said yes.

The next day I decided to be breezy and noncommittal with my first letter, and began it on plain ruled notebook paper. It

was casual and jokey and contained careful allusions to the
absorbing things I did in my spare time and how worn out I
was from constant social and collegiate activity.

I put it aside to finish, and three days later Jason's letter
arrived in the mail. I was alone when it came, and I marveled
at his last name, which I hadn't known: Winslow. This new
bit of information reshaped my mental image of him somehow, giving him the burnished legitimacy of someone with
a background and a lineage. I carried the letter upstairs and
opened it on my bed. It was sealed with a sticker depicting a wolf's face with the caption *PROTECT NATURAL
HABITATS.*

The letter began:

> *I know you were supposed to write first, but I am letting you off
> the hook because there were just a few things I wanted to say right
> away. First of all I want to say "thank you" for talking to me. Like
> I said it was the best conversation I had all break. I'm glad to be back
> in WI but I wish we could have hung out more, it would have been
> cool to see you again and get a hug before I left.*

The rest of the letter talked about how interesting and
smart he thought I was and how glad he'd been to meet me.
He spelled some words wrong and his grammar was sometimes off, but I didn't care. I sat on my bed and read the letter three times, studying the boyish untidiness of his
handwriting: that all-caps kind of male handwriting that
looked like a bunch of sticks leaning into each other. The
whole letter oozed a guileless freewheeling candor that
warmed me; there was no visible calculation, no orchestrated

indifference, and yet his eagerness didn't feel desperate. It had a loose and shaggy innocence. It was as though he had never had anything bad happen to him.

For the first time in a long time, I was hit with the girlish impulse to disclose. I wanted to show the letter to someone and shamelessly, dotingly analyze it, but there was nobody. But I had to do something. This pent-up squealy responsiveness needed to be discharged. I went to my desk and took out my spiral notebook. Next to the shambling, unassuming sincerity of his words, my careful letter-in-progress seemed cold-blooded, dismissive, glaringly false in its little evasions and self-protective witticisms.

I turned the page in the notebook and began a new letter. I wrote:

Last year at the East Town Street Fair, a woman read my palm. She said, "Keep your money. Just be young and creative and full of ideas, and that's payment enough."

Then she told me I had had a close brush with the other world but had survived and will live to be at least sixty or seventy. I will someday choose between two men. Someone will achieve great things because of knowing me, things that would not have been possible without my existence. That's all.

I tell you this because I want to subvert it. I don't want that to be my life. For a long time I believed that all sufferings are written in the stars and that their absence would cause the delicate balance of the universe to be disrupted. I believed everything happened for a reason. Originally I believed in fate because I was Catholic, and then because I was pagan. When I was Catholic I was obsessed with original sin and when I was a pagan I was obsessed with past lives. Basically they embody the same principle: you are to blame for everything that happens to you.

When you told me about putting the radio collar on the female wolf, I envied you. I want to find a beautiful wild thing and track it, be able to tell if it's still alive from hundreds of miles away, be able to know I had once touched a killer while she was unconscious, briefly and vulnerably harmless for the first time in her life. I keep thinking of the wolf waking up in the snow hours later like a creature coming out of a spell, feeling that something about her was different but not knowing why, shaking the snow off her fur and running back into the trees, irreversibly changed, connected to someone now. And never knowing it. But on some cellular level I think she does know. Maybe that's why she went so far away.

One thing the palm-reader said was true: I did have a brush with death. I tried to starve myself when I was 19. It was a project. It was hypnotic at first, like I was building something—or, more accurately, disassembling it—and I took pride in how it frightened people. How they were actually scared of me. Then I got scared of myself, because I couldn't stop it. But they put me in a hospital and eventually I did.

That was when I became a pagan. I figured I had tried to starve myself because of the Catholic asceticism I'd been raised with, and I wanted a religion that was softer and more forgiving. But it wasn't really. The pagans thought you were responsible for your own unhappiness because you chose each successive life based on the lessons you hadn't learned yet in your previous lives. A guy tried to have sex with me once in his tent at a Rainbow Festival. He kept saying, "Let me, just let me," in this gentle voice, but afterwards I had bruises on my legs and arms, even though I managed to get away from him (I was sober, he was on mushrooms and a bunch of other stuff). When I told my friend Teal she said, "It's just because you're so beautiful, Katrina." Which is basically what the Catholics would have said, except not as nicely. I never even fit in with the ones who weren't spiritual at all, who just hung around for the drum circles and pot. I wanted to be part of it so badly, but I couldn't. I could wear the clothes, even sew the clothes, but I wasn't one of them.

Choose life, said the Catholics. Choose life, said the pagans. I finally am, but not in the way either creed intended. I don't want to know every little thing that'll happen to me up until the day I die. I don't want to follow the plan of a higher power. I think that meeting you, singling you out and asking you for something, was the first step toward a new way of being. And I am changed now. I am touched, and I walk into the woods knowing it.

I wrote more. I said his body was familiar to me even though we had just met. I said that being with him felt safe and dream-like. I talked about the hollow of his throat and the nobility of his collarbone. I stuffed the letter into an envelope without rereading it, sealed it with a PETA sticker, and mailed it that same day.

For the days I imagined it would take to get from Michigan to Wisconsin, I fantasized about Jason's life being changed by my words. Of him marveling at how smart and insightful I was, my clever turns of phrase, the forthrightness of my disclosures. I imagined his reverent recognition of the wily survivor in me, my gritty transcendence. I imagined his awe.

But his awe was apparently so great that he couldn't write back. I waited and waited. I put myself on hold and each day was terribly long, rubbery with tedium, humiliation settling in as I began to realize he wasn't going to respond.

After two weeks of waiting I was in the living room, unable to sleep, when Rachel came in and flopped down on the couch next to me. She looked at me blankly.

"I don't think that guy's going to write me back," I said without looking at her.

"Well," she said, "why do you think that?"

I folded my hands in my lap. "I just know. I have a feeling."

Rachel sat there for a while. Then she gripped my shoulder and sort of shook it. It wasn't a tender, there-there pat. Her fingers were bony and they closed around the ball-and-joint socket like one of those metal claws in vending machines. I blinked at her.

"Do you remember in high school," she said, "when I wrote that research paper on the Jonestown massacre, and Mrs. Healy told us to start a paper with a first line that would grab hold of the reader, and so I started mine with, *How could this have happened?!?* And for the rest of the year you'd just randomly turn to me every time the least little thing happened— like the lunch line was out of corndogs, or I was low on gas—and blurt out, 'How could this have happened?!?' in this melodramatic crazy voice? Do you remember that?"

"Yeah," I said. "I guess."

"That was so funny," Rachel said. Now her voice sounded far away and distantly marveling. "I was thinking about that the other day. How funny you always were."

We sat there a couple minutes before I realized she was crying.

"Rachel," I said. "Oh, no." I put my arm around her, but she curled tightly into herself like a rolled-up beetle, her body a hard brittle arc in blue jersey pajamas, tremoring just a little. I kept patting her, aghast. I tried to remember an earlier version of myself—my adolescent self, slouched low in a series of plastic chairs, wearing pants that were too baggy, mocking everything—and I knew what would make Rachel feel better. She wanted me to make fun of her. But I couldn't. It was like a spell I'd forgotten how to cast. After a while I stopped patting her and she stopped crying.

A few days later she told me she was moving out. She and Josh decided to get a place together next semester. I said okay. I told her she could take the toaster and can opener and the green couch we'd picked out together at Goodwill. "That's awesome of you," she said. This conversation—over cups of tea in the sunny kitchen, both of our faces strangely careworn in the wash of sunlight—felt like we were in a movie about women who were at a crossroads, a serene our-paths-have-diverged crossroads, but at the same time it didn't feel like that at all.

Well into the new semester, I couldn't stop imagining Jason in the snowy forests of Wisconsin: tracking wolves with a faceless cadre of fellow biologists, peering at paw prints and scat, and, later, in some rustic Wisconsin pub with antlers on the wall and patrons in feed caps, half feral from his prolonged proximity to wildness, telling his friends about me. Quoting the letter and shaking his head and laughing, a little sheepishly. Then shutting up because he felt bad. Then tipping a long glass down his throat, averting his eyes, studying the antlers. And as I replayed what I'd written in my head and saw my revelations as self-important, performative, my metaphors strained, the crude obviousness of my need and self-ennobling loneliness, I cringed.

Tom asked me about him once.

"I don't correspond with people who can't spell," I told him.

"I love your standards," he said. "That's so you. Forget compatibility; literacy is the deal-breaker. Literacy *is* compatibility."

I remembered my ex-boyfriend's voice over the phone from London, where he was studying abroad. How he said, "I don't even know who you *are*."

"Then you're an idiot," I told him from across the ocean.

Rachel left and I put out an ad for a roommate. *Please be vegetarian*, the ad said. Tom started dating a girl, Jada, who worked with him in the independent bookstore. She had an angelic moon-face and she didn't like me. She told Tom I was unfriendly. After a few months he decided to move in with her.

"Great," I told him. "But I'm not visiting you in that place." Jada lived with six roommates in a co-op in East Town. The co-op was for people brought together by their mutual devotion to minimalism. They painted the walls bright, accusatory colors and what little furniture they had was eggshell-shaped, tilted, and hard. In order to be admitted, Tom had to get rid of every extraneous scrap of comfort he owned.

A week before the move, I went to Tom's apartment to sift through his stuff and see if there was anything I wanted. I knew there wouldn't be. But I was bored.

"In my room," he called out when I knocked.

As I entered the kitchen, the first thing I noticed was that Jada had tacked a note to Tom's refrigerator. It said:

All the things that rustle in my brain
When I wake up and see you smiling there's quiet
And calm
Love

Jada's handwriting was fluid and looped. I looked at the paper and felt the pang of being outside of something: not only the intimacy of the message but the womanly elegance of its execution, its curvaceous authority, graceful and almost musky with privacy, splashed across the bland beige of the fridge like a bloody handprint.

"Hey, Tom," I called out from the kitchen. "Tell me something."

"Huh?" he called.

I said, "Were you ever jealous of Barrett?"

Barrett was a charismatic hippie guy with long dreadlocks, a friend of Teal's. He read Russian literature. We made out once but he never called me afterward.

I wandered into Tom's bedroom, where he was sifting through piles of old magazines. He tossed a wrinkly copy of *Utne Reader* at me.

"Should I recycle all this?" he said. His back was to me. "I just want to put it in a garbage bag on the side of the road."

He started whipping magazines in my direction without turning around, occasionally making whizzing plane noises. I ducked so they wouldn't hit me. Then he stopped.

"No, I was never jealous of Barrett," he finally said, without facing me. He was still rummaging, or pretending to. "If I was jealous of anyone, it was that guy you slept with. That blond guy. *That* guy."

My stomach lurched sickeningly. "Why?" I said.

Tom turned around and looked at me. "I think," he said, "I thought I could have given you what you wanted that night. Because he obviously couldn't. He had his chance and he couldn't. It was, like, what a waste that guy was."

I rolled the magazine into a tube and unrolled it.

"But it doesn't matter now," Tom said.

He turned back around and resumed rifling, tossing old shoes out of the way, stacking vinyl records in a messy pile. His vintage cowboy shirt rode up in the back, and I could see his ribs. I joined him, just to have something to do with my hands, rifling through old yearbooks and magazines. Then I came across something thin and weathered with the cover ripped off.

I held it up in front of Tom's face until he had to look at me. His expression changed.

"Oh my God," he said. He brought his hand to his mouth in what seemed like genuine embarrassment. "I totally forgot I had that."

I didn't say anything. He kept talking. His voice got faster and higher.

"I think," he said, "someone gave me this a million years ago for a joke. Look at their hair!"

He opened the magazine to a spread of two women and a man. The man was on a bed, with one of the women crouching over his face and the other one sucking his dick. All three of them had feathered hair and expressions of feral, narrow-eyed concentration. The setting looked like a not-very-clean room in a chain motel.

Tom and I settled down side by side. We leaned against the

closet door and flipped through the magazine, laughing at the overheated captions and bad hair, the garish makeup and gratuitous alliteration of the accompanying text. The men all looked angry, almost demonic, and the women wore identical expressions of slack-jawed, sultry indolence.

"This is the saddest thing I've ever seen," I said. It kind of was. It occurred to me that people don't look good while they're having sex.

I took the magazine from him and flipped to a spread featuring a dark-haired young woman wearing tight, high-waisted white jeans and strutting through an empty city street covered with graffiti. At the top of the page, in black writing meant to look like spray-painted tagging, was the headline "A Special Anal Section."

"Here," I said. "Let me regale you."

Tom started giggling.

"Shut up," I said. Then I began to read the text. *"I was walking down the street when I saw this hot bitch swinging her ass all over the place. She was definitely ready for action. I knew I had to have that ass."*

I was reading in a mock-breathless voice for a while. Then I started reading in my normal voice. I could have been in grade school when the teacher made us go around the room taking turns reading from the text, and we were all careful not to sound too animated.

"She told me, There's nothing my ass wants more than a big, hard cock," I read. *"Yours will do nicely."*

I kept going, through the scene-setting preamble and into the actual sex part, which was, like all the sex depicted thus far, portrayed as merely the long-delayed expression of some ancient, displaced rage. Then, just as I was about to narrate the mutually reached climax, I realized Tom's body was held rigidly away from me, like Rachel's that night on the couch. His eyes tipped toward the ceiling and he sat stock-still. I might as well have been reading to an empty room. I put the magazine down.

"Are you aroused?" I said. My voice was saccharine and almost congratulatory: the same tone I'd used on Trina, the one-year-old girl I used to babysit for in high school, whenever she mastered some developmental milestone. *Are you walking all by yourself?*

"Do you need a moment alone?" I asked Tom. He didn't answer. He just turned his face away from me, toward the wall. I could feel the heat on his cheek and I remembered how he'd touched my thigh in his truck: the frustrated, foreshortened slap of his hand, bouncing. I put the magazine on the floor next to him. Then I got up and went into the living room.

From Tom's couch I could see two kids on swings. They were twisting the metal chains together so that they could rock back and forth fast as they unraveled. It was then—sitting alone on the only remaining piece of furniture in Tom's apartment as he jerked off in his bedroom and those kids spun below me, suspended at the end of their long chains like marionettes— that I thought about, for the first time, how I'd lied to Jason. And I'd known all along but still the knowledge felt new, and stunning. The palm-reader thing was true but none of the rest. I was never anorexic. Tactless strangers regularly asked me if I was; but I'd always been naturally skinny. And all I could remember about Catholic school were the hymns and laughing with Rachel all the time and how an ancient priest said, *Just try to be nicer*, when I confessed the sin of mocking some poor girl's hair. The guy at the Rainbow Festival didn't try to rape me. Maybe he would have, but I never went into his tent with him. I would never have been that stupid. And even though I knew these things weren't the exact truth, they were a variation of it, and they felt true as I wrote them down. And they still felt like the truth—as if on some deeper, irreproachable level, those incidents hatched me like a newborn chick and I'd crawled from the wreckage of them with a bright new face. They had to have happened, because if they hadn't, how could I explain the unhappy accident of myself?

A few minutes later Tom came out, very slowly.

"Was that weird?" he said. "To do that?"

I shrugged. "It doesn't matter."

"It's getting late," he said. "I can give you a ride home."

I almost told him. I almost said, *I'm a liar*. Then I didn't. I knew he would listen intently and end up applauding my insights and offering his own theories, and I didn't feel like going through that.

So what I said instead was, too pointedly for my meaning to be misconstrued, "Don't take me home."

it sounds like you're feeling

Someone has spiked their meds with poison and hijacked their dreams. Sleep eludes them. They are haunted by long-lost bathroom graffiti. They see shadows shaped like the continent of Africa. They have no one to talk to and they can't stand themselves anymore and you have to get that fucker on the phone, they say, this is a job for a professional, this is what the fucker is *paid for*. And when you explain that you can't do that, that you can only page a caseworker if it's life-or-death, they say, "Okay, I'm going to kill myself." Then you page the caseworker. Time after time you walk right into it: Charlie Brown with the football.

It happens so often that the caseworkers complain. Any altruistic inclination they ever had has been strangled by red tape and buried under multicolored forms in triplicate. They don't care that you're an intern. You have been exposed as

a bastion of incompetence, easily undone by the vagaries of
the insane, their needs and their wiles. The caseworkers hate
you and you cannot blame them. Especially after the seven-
hundred-pound man.

Which, incidentally, is not your fault. It is the fault of your
supervisor, Tyler, and his vain attempts to mentor you in the
finer points of helpline etiquette. It is the fault of Tyler wend-
ing in and out of the rows of phone cubicles with the compact wariness of a fleshy, tubular fish, tensely expectant of
denunciation as always, coming up to you and saying, "You
can't give in to them," during a rare lull in the insane population's siege. It is the fault of Tyler draping one arm over the
wall of your cubicle with his other hand on his hip, his hair
sharply sculpted and smelling of product and his fingers drum-
ming the pebbled-gray cubicle wall inches above a yellowing
postcard claiming that life is 10 percent what happens to you
and 90 percent what you do with what happens to you.

It is the fault of Tyler saying, "The caseworkers are on call
twenty-four/seven. They need *relief*."

Then he says, "The cardinal rule is CYA. Remember?"

This stands for Cover Your Ass, a dictum that caused
homophobic snickers during training. Your training-session
notes contained phrases like *MIRRORING IS ESSENTIAL*
and *NO ADVICE!!!*

When your phone shrills, Tyler gives the top of the cubicle two rapid-fire taps and motions for you to pick up. "I'll
be on the extension," he whispers.

You pick up: "Hello, Keystone Mental Health Helpline,"
in the neutral and nonstigmatizing tone you have practiced.

"Hello," the caller says. At first you think he must have

dialed the wrong number, because his voice is weighted with a burdensome mindfulness that is not at all insane. He sounds like someone calling to complain, regretfully and evenly, about shoddy service.

He is silent for a long moment, and you blurt out, "What can I do for you?"

The caller says, "I don't know. Nothing, I guess. I guess I just wanted to talk to someone."

You say, "What would you like to talk about?"

"I weigh seven hundred pounds," the man says. He clears his throat, and instantly you visualize him hunched at a kitchen table with a chicken leg in his hand, even though he doesn't sound like he's eating. In the kitchen where you place him, all the lights are off.

You ask him how he feels. He says he can barely move. He is sick of living with his mother. He is sick of not having a job. He is lonely. He is afraid he is going to die soon. He feels sorry for his heart. "Is that weird?" he says. "That I feel sorry for my own heart? Like it's an animal trying to pull a combine. It's too small for what it has to do." His voice trails.

You say, "Have you seen a doctor?" You hear an urgent rustling from Tyler's vicinity, and in a few moments a Post-it is waving frantically above his cubicle wall, emblazoned with the word *JUDGMENTAL!!!* in black Sharpie.

The seven-hundred-pound man says, "I hate doctors. They judge me."

Tyler's Post-it dances mockingly across the aisle. You ask the man if he ever takes warm baths.

He is silent. Then he says, "I can't fit in the tub. I wash with a handheld nozzle thing."

You say, "What about a nice walk?"

"Are you making fun of me?" he says. His voice is sodden with resignation. "I can't move very far."

Then something hits you in the head. It turns out to be a paper airplane, lobbed by Tyler and fashioned from a training handout entitled "It Sounds Like You're Feeling" . . . and listing dozens of adjectives depicting the full gamut of human emotions. They are listed alphabetically, from *anxious* to *wretched*. Some of them aren't lone words but phrases, states of being, like *worn down* and *all worked up*. You hear the caller's belabored breathing and are seized with an irrational certainty that he will die of massive heart failure if you don't say something, so you blurt out, "It sounds like you're feeling . . ."

You feverishly scan the list but you cannot find a word to adequately fill in this blank. You can't bring yourself to say any of them: not *disempowered*, not *scared*, not *restless*, not *hopeful*. Nothing fits. And you can feel the seven-hundred-pound man on the other side of this silence, breathing in the dark, lowering his fist with its imaginary food, waiting to be described.

"Are you there?" he says.

"Um," you say, rustling the sheet. "Just a minute. It sounds like . . ." and you stop, because you couldn't possibly sound more like you're reading from a piece of paper if you tried.

"Oh my God," the man says, disgust and hurt stiffening his voice. "Are you reading from something?"

Then the line goes dead. Tyler's cube fairly shakes with consternation. And that is what does it. No matter how vociferously you argue that the seven-hundred-pound caller was not an insane person and had no caseworker, that he was an unknown entity, a rogue element, one of the rare breed of callers who found the hotline through the Yellow Pages or a bus advertisement and not the usual social-service network, and therefore could not be dealt with in the same fashion as the standard helpline clientele, Tyler and the codirector, Kara, are adamant. You are not psychologically equipped to deal with the chronically impaired.

They frame it as a learning experience.

"There are so many mental-health professionals on this campus," Tyler says, "and they have *all* mastered the art of Empathic Listening. All you have to do is talk. And observe how they respond. Let them model it for you."

Kara adds, "Healers need healing, too. The world doesn't need another social worker who hasn't dealt with her own issues."

Which is why, on a sleety Saturday in February, you rise at seven a.m., drink your tea, vacuum your apartment, and board the bus to the university's Counseling Center.

"Would you prefer to talk to a male or female counselor?" asks the middle-aged receptionist. She is wearing a novelty sweater spattered with bears and hearts. You say you don't care. She hands you a sheaf of forms to fill out and you leave blank all inquiries regarding sex, interpersonal relationships, and the ordeals and rites of passage of your formative years. You don't want anything going on your record. Then the receptionist says, "Here's your counselor, dear."

A large fluffy dog, the color of autumnal leaves, enters the room. It pauses and wags its tail. Then you notice that it is attached to a tall wiry-haired man who is following the dog

toward you, taking small, deliberate steps like a man afraid to
break through ice, and smiling in your general direction with
the tentative, adjustable aim of the blind.

"Hello," the man says. His head serenely immobile. "This
here is Monty, and I'm Colin."

He comes to a halt about two feet off your right side and
extends his palm straight in front of him at a forty-degree
angle from your torso, and at first you think he is making
some sort of faith-healing gesture like a televangelist. Then
you realize that he is trying to shake your hand and is missing
his target. You reposition yourself until his hand brushes
yours. He seizes it. It occurs to you that interacting with the
blind is akin to perpetually letting a child win: a series of soft
lobs, no strategic feinting, all energies concentrated into making your body a stationary, stolid bull's-eye. You have never
spoken to a blind person before. The dog puts its head
between its paws.

"Why don't we head back to my office?" the blind man
says. You have heard that blind people's remaining senses are
supernaturally heightened and you wonder if he can tell
there's something wrong with you by registering the whorls
of your palm, the texture of your skin, if he is finding evi-
dence of congenital defects in the invisible emanations from
your pores, signs of incapacity that will go on your record,
and you fear that he is going to hold your hand all the way
down the hall to his office like a lover, but he lets go. The
dog leads the way into a small, windowless room with beige
walls. You distribute your limbs on a steel-armed blue leath-
erette club chair that appears to have been salvaged from an
airport. Colin carefully lowers himself onto an identical seat

across from you. The dog flops down with a sound like someone uncorked it.

"Now," Colin says. He is still smiling but his eyes are hidden behind dark glasses in which you can see yourself, miniaturized and doubled, balled tightly in the chair. "Before we talk about why you came in today, I suggest doing a relaxing breathing exercise for a couple minutes, just to put you at ease. Because you seem very anxious and upset. Do you want to give it a try?"

"Okay," you say. You stare at the grids of glen plaid on Colin's shirt, the silvery cap of his hair, and his careful, stout fingers as he puts his staff down and leads you in a series of deep breaths. But you disobey his command to close your eyes. You absorb visual stimuli with impunity, cataloguing madly, *I see that and that and that*, while you swallow air in slow gulps. You wonder if his eyes are actually closed behind his glasses.

After a few moments, Colin laughs. "Listen," he says softly, indicating the dog. "She's doing it, too."

Indeed, the fluffy dog is breathing with the same measured rhythm as her master. You laugh, too. Then you feel like you want to cry. You are seized by a clinging, insistent hunch that your sudden teariness is entirely due to the fact that you're in a room with a dog and a blind person. Because it's unexpected, you tell yourself: the double vulnerability of them, their twinned soft mildness, how you can't stop wondering what they'd do if the dog got cataracts: would another, smaller creature be assigned to it, something with excellent eyesight, a trained raptor maybe, that would lead the way with the dog behind it and Colin behind the dog, the caravan growing and growing as they all aged and deteriorated, on and on like a series of Russian nesting dolls? Your thoughts are making no sense.

Then Colin asks why you came in. You say you're having trouble handling the calls at your internship. You're having trouble sticking to the script, is how you put it.

Colin says, "Why don't you give me some context here? How did you get into social work?" He folds his hands. His voice, so gently inquisitive, has managed to leach the question of all idle curiosity and righteous expectation of an answer, but he doesn't sound disinterested either. You wonder how he does that.

You say, "I want to help people." This is what you always say.

Colin says, "Well, you can't give help without getting help. It's the natural order of things."

He then asks you to ponder how the people on the help-line are helping *you*. You try to humor him. You say that the helpline callers at least make you feel you're not *that* messed up. That as lonely as you sometimes get, at least you're not out of your mind. Even in your darkest hours you don't get desperate enough to call a complete stranger and unleash the thorny devil of your id, expose your most shameful recesses, only to be told to take a bath.

He says, "What do you do, then? In your darkest hours?"

You pause. You read, you tell him. You draw. You call your mom. You try to focus on the positive.

For a while Colin says nothing. He does not advise you to take a bath. He does not tell you how you are feeling. You and Colin and Monty sit in silence in this room with its institutional sandstone carpet, and you wonder if Colin is asleep behind his dark glasses. Despite the dearth of Empathic Listening taking place you begin to feel physically pacified by the sheer monochromatic weight of his nonresponse. Then Colin gets up and stretches out his hand. You are afraid he is going to try to feel your face, like blind characters on TV are always doing. But he simply coaxes your hand from your lap and holds it with an air of neutrally solicitous consideration, like a fragile item he is thinking of buying and is careful not to break. He says, "I hope we can continue to work together." He uses your name.

It is not, as Tyler would say, a cathartic disclosure. On the way out the door your glance snags on Monty staring up from her place on the rug. Her black eyes are brimming with confusion, guarded hope, and what you can only identify as profound canine concern, the concern of a companion animal trained to not only sniff out one's weakness but to worry about it.

There are secular construction-paper hearts on Keystone's windows: hearts without thorns or bleeding gashes, hearts that are not aflame. A tall male intern with a thatch of wild dark hair has begun to daily diagnose your mental state— "You look relaxed today," he'll say, or "You seem well rested this morning," and then stare at you with a close-lipped smile that seems to slide sideways off his face. At first you think he is practicing his helpline banter, but he says these things to no one else. At training sessions he slouches low in his chair and stares up at Tyler with his mouth open and his small brown eyes insolently vacant. On the phone with the insane he speaks from an insulated trough far back in his throat, consonants callused, vowels cocooned, mummifying his voice so thoroughly that you cannot tell if he is very kind or very cruel. You bump up vocally against him and feel the shock of your words absorbed and muted, and it makes you want to raise your voice, ram the big cloddy sandbag of his personality until it swings back at you, suddenly lethal.

After a grueling call rife with helpline-speak, the tall young man habitually leans over your cubicle and hisses something along the lines of, "It sounds like you're feeling . . . *fucking whacked out of your mind*!" Then he will pick up the ringing phone and recommend a bath, a walk, a favorite TV show in his husky, blunted voice.

On Valentine's Day you get a call from a man who says, "Yeah, is this the helpline?"

"Yes," you say.

"Well, good," he says, "because I need some *help*." He sounds like a slightly insane Barry White.

"With what?" you say. It strikes you that the paper hearts aren't red, but the dusky maroon of a smoker's lung.

The caller says, "I need a massage. I got a kink in my neck, baby."

"That is inappropriate," you say. "This helpline is not for your own personal titillation. But a hot bath may alleviate your muscle tension." You disconnect. Tyler gives you a thumbs-up. But when you relate this anecdote to the wild-haired young man, he erupts into a round of laughter like a weapon detonating. "It sounds like you're feeling . . . *pervy*," he snorts, pretending to consult the worksheet, and leans over to knead your collarbone with surprising force. You brace yourself and let him.

Then he says, "You look happy today." He strides away.

Later that week you tell Colin that you don't understand why the tall young man keeps saying these things to you. Are you unwittingly emitting some sort of contented essence, and if so, what opening does it come from and how can you seal it?

"Is that really the issue?" Colin says. He is terrible at this. He is not mirroring; he is not empathizing; he is posing open-ended and loaded questions that Tyler has explicitly forbidden. *You are to wean them off the line with a minimum of confessional discourse.*

"Is what the issue?" you say. "That I can't tell what people are feeling, or even what I'm feeling? Isn't that the whole issue? Isn't that the whole reason I'm here?"

You have never been this rude to anyone before.

What if, you demand of Colin as the twin lagoons of his lenses regard you with limpid impassivity, the insanity you detect over the phone hides a deep and inarguable logic? What if you are mirroring the wrong emotions, and therefore not mirroring at all, what if you are reflecting callers' moods back at them through a funhouse mirror, declaring, "It sounds like you're feeling miserable," when in fact they are capering, swooning with joy? When you were a philosophy major for two months you pondered this: the subjectivity of all things, the tail-chasing, Mad Hatter gibberish of theory, and it made you dizzy and peaked.

Colin says, "Maybe this man is interested in you. And he just doesn't know what to say to you."

"No," you respond. "Nobody is 'interested' in me." You pick two loose threads off Colin's rug.

Now he'll ask about sex. You knew this would happen sooner or later.

Colin says, "How can you know that for sure? How would it feel to you if he *was* interested?"

"It doesn't matter," you say, "because that is not the case."

He sits there. He is waiting, you can tell, for you to crack. A blind man with a dog who is beginning to resemble him— frowsy, leaking sighs and grunts, unnervingly mild—is asking you to justify your highly dysfunctional attitude toward your own romantic viability and you will not do it, you will not trot out the stock villains, you will not rehash the smug trite- ness of it all because it's been done, it's old: even the night- mares have the stale odor of a textbook. If you knew Braille maybe you could tell him, punch in that violent, stabbing Sanskrit, let him trace it with his fingers as though feeling his way through a maze. If he learned it first with his body there would be a time lag in which his brain processed the balky and inadequate translation, and you could make your escape with ease and grace.

"What do you see?" you blurt out. Colin turns the mir- rored black ovals of his glasses in your direction. "Pardon?" he says.

"I mean," you say, "is it all black, like shoe-polish-black? Or do you see the outlines of things, in shadow? Or lights?"

For a moment he is silent. His mouth opens and closes. You guess at what's going on in his mind: ethical wrestling, pedagogical ghosts at war with all that is spontaneously human. You know he wants to respond. You know how your question sounds: not idly curious but taut, an outthrust, naked ligament. His glasses are pointed straight ahead and the black portholes look strangely visionary, hyperintelligent, Martian-like. He licks his lips.

"That's not what we're here to talk about," he says firmly. Monty stirs at his feet.

You sit up straight. In the thirty minutes that remain, you tell Colin all about the majors you've had so far and why you dropped them. You spent a semester as a kinesiology major because you liked the idea of the actual existence of something called a Gait and Posture Lab. But you quit because of the phraseology: that euphemistic fascist language of the body, its lofty obfuscation of the simplest and humblest movements and functions. Then you became a geology major. Until the professor showed earthquake footage in class and you replayed it every night in your dreams, your shaky feet tightroping the molten seam that rose up, livid and flaring as a welt, as the ground split open. Then for a short while you studied English lit but the similes made you give it up: all that gratuitous shape-shifting of the familiar, all those groundless comparisons. You like to think that you stumbled into social work not randomly, but as a culmination of the impulses that had been driving you all along. You wanted to keep people's bodies moving fluidly, then to protect them from geological disasters, then to understand them better by increasing your fluency in human passions via classic works of literature. And finally you realized that it was a luxury to worry about any of those things, that the real work involved life's necessities: shelter, food, sanity. The management of cases.

Colin says, "What else is necessary for life?"

"Oh. Health," you say. Time is up. You start to drift toward the door. "I forgot health."

As you cross the threshold Colin says, "It's like an ultrasound. Or an EKG."

You freeze midstep. Then you know what he means.

The huge black voids of his lenses turn slowly toward you. "That's what it's like," he says. "Staticky. Wavy."

You stand there in the doorway. "Oh," you say. The clock ticks. Monty sighs.

He adds, "And if the lights are on or off, I can tell."

You find a book in the Keystone break room called *Soul Recovery*, and you keep it in your bag for a week before perusing its ungrammatical and boldface-heavy content. Then you read it while taking calls, utilizing the "It Sounds Like You're Feeling" worksheet as a bookmark.

"I'm telling you," an insane woman says, "they're going to evict me. They're down there plotting to evict me, because I'm closing my refrigerator door too hard and they can hear it and what if it flies off its hinges? I can't open the damn thing to get my meds. Because if I open it, then I'd have to close it, and they'll kick me out for closing it too hard!"

The back cover of *Soul Recovery* says:

Are you interested in a tangible,
Action-oriented plan of
recovery from trauma
GUARENTEED to diminish FIFTEEN YEARS
of recovery work to a

REASONABLE AMOUNT OF YOUR TIME?
Of course you are.

You tell the woman, "It sounds like you're feeling worried."

"Don't you tell me how I'm feeling," she snaps. "I know how I'm feeling and I'm sick of this 'it sounds like you're feeling' bullshit."

"Maybe you would relax if you took a nice, hot bath," you say. You flip to a page in *Soul Recovery* that says, *The glory is there and when the source is tapped, healing waters springforth.* You have no idea what this means.

The insane woman says, "I'm sick of taking baths. Why is everyone I talk to here always telling me to take a fucking bath? Am I that dirty?"

"We're here to listen," you tell her. "That's what we do." It is odd to be so unaffected by her anger, to resist the impulse to confer lucidity and righteousness upon her simply because she is raging at you. You are learning to love the sweet airless bloat of unconditional dismissal. The safeness of sloganeering. You may have found your major.

Later, the wild-haired young man sidles over to your cubicle and says, "You look no-nonsense today." You smile up at him. When he swipes at the nape of your neck you are beyond flinching. There is an absence of something, a happy void like the shiny circle of Colin's glasses, and it occurs to you that your soul has not recovered but has instead simply left, and you wish it well. It occurs to you that the soul is just another body—only sheerer and with fewer points of entrance or exit—and yours has tiptoed, giddily impish as a truant, away from the flesh puppet. You expected it to hurt more than this, or at least to be accompanied by a ripping sound.

Tyler strolls by, underarms saturated, and says, "You two crazy kids."

Officially, you know it is the alcohol that does it. The two-for-one happy hour at the tall man's chosen drinking establishment. You know it peels your body into layers like the mica schist of your long-lost geology lab. You know it turns you into a walking violation of natural law: simultaneously diluted and distilled. You know it's the alcohol and that is the story you will stick to later, but you also know that you want him to touch you, or at least to touch some part of you, while leaving your glowing and furnace-bright center, the flaming coal of your selfhood, completely alone. And when he picks up your hand across the table of balled napkins and moisture rings, and drives your vacated body to a place with a bed and gets on top of you as you are lying on it, and when he touches your neck and tells you it's a pretty neck, all your layers collide, flailing for integration in the sleeve of your body, and you are too present suddenly, afraid of what he wants from you and why. You wish for Colin. You wish for Monty. Right then and there you want the predictable and temperate decency of them, the finite and bloodless parameters of what they expect from you; you want them to come into the room and firmly, gently tell the young man that you have to go now, and you would follow them out the door with the same sense of limp gratitude, the same eleventh-hour reprieve, that you felt when you were little and your mother would unexpectedly pick you up from ballet class early.

"Can you go slow?" you ask the dark-haired man. Then you realize you don't know his last name.

"Okay," he says. He adjusts himself and he says in his stubbed, congested voice, sounding like someone whose bad cold is really turning him on, "Tell me how it feels."

He could be kidding. You are unschooled in the subtleties of sexual banter. For a moment you freeze: How does it feel? Is it supposed to feel any different than it ever has? And what if it does feel different? Must you now define it? As if in answer, there is a coalescing inside you: a solemn alignment of particles, a closing of ranks. You glaze over with a canny lubricity. His weight is on you. You don't need to answer any questions. You do not need to run out of the room. You can move in the ways people are supposed to move. You can reach for what juts out, taut and unforgiving as a rip cord, between his body and yours.

———

Colin has a habit of kneading the round top of his walking stick like a fretful king with a scepter. As the therapeutic hour progresses, this tic supersedes every other identifying trait.

"Here's what I want you to think about," he says. "Why do you think you shut off during this moment of intimacy?"

You watch his hands writhe across the knob of the stick with sniveling gentleness. For the tenth time this morning you feel it: the queasy sloughing sensation, the wave of erosion exposing a tender gully in your lower abdomen. You have felt yourself slowly diminishing all morning—since the tall man drove you here and dropped you off with a diffident hug—and you thought it was a good thing, a result of having touched another human being in a sensual manner for the first time since your long-lost days as an urban studies major. You felt sleeker, as though a primordial overhead had been cut, rendering you cleanly functional as an animal and almost as innocent. Walking into Colin's office, you were struck by an urge to announce reactivated kinship with the rest of the world. And you told him. And he put his hand on his chin and rubbed, which is what he does when he's puzzling over why you have done the things you have done.

"I thought you'd be glad," you say.

Colin said, "Is it for my sake that you did this?" His voice is exaggeratedly incredulous.

He rubs the top of the stick. And as you watch him, you are suddenly deflated by the fact that you can do shameful things with one person and disclose them to another and neither one is more than a collage of idiosyncrasies: restless hands, a smell of smoky cologne, a thicket of hair on the lower back. You have come to rely solely on traits like these in order to tell people apart. It gets far too complicated to classify them according to whatever nonsensical thing they did with or to you.

"I'm only here," you say, "because the helpline is making me. I'm here as an observer of your technique. Which, incidentally, is totally judgmental and would completely get me fired if I used it."

"Well, tell me this, then," Colin says, shifting in his chair. "If someone called your helpline and related to you the episode you just described to me, what would you tell them?"

You fold your arms. "To take a bath," you say, "or a walk."

"And that's it?"

"Then I would tell them what it sounds like they're feeling."

"And," Colin says with infernal cleverness, hunching forward with his lenses slipping down his nose, "what would that feeling be?"

Monty snorts on the rug, stretching her hind legs. For a moment you can't feel your face.

"Take off your glasses," you tell Colin. Something greased and ruthless stirs in the hollow of your belly.

He stiffens. "No," he says. He opens his mouth and closes it. You hear the moist squish of his lips separating.

"Come on," you say. "I want to see your eyes."

There's a silence. Then he says, "I'm sorry, but I think I need to ask you to leave," the words running together a bit, nervous, jerking his head up and around as if trying to elude the lens of an invisible camera, a useless instinctual holdover from a time when he could see, and this is how you know that he has not been blind all his life.

You stand up. This doesn't really matter, because you know how to pave over such things. You know how to pull yourself together and walk out of a room. Walking out of rooms is one of your favorite activities.

Your hand hovers over Colin's body and you wonder if his heightened senses pick up the intention of touch. You suddenly want to touch everyone on earth—not tenderly, not sensually, but in the role of prankish mythological imp, the kind that disappears after tripping up legs, spearing hearts with arrows. Just to jar every stolid hipbone and free-floating coccyx in the world. You feel you have a license to do that now.

But at the last second you stoop down and pet Monty

instead, despite the sign she wears explicitly forbidding petting. The ruff around her neck is coarse and thick, separating into blond spears that are dark at the roots. Her black eyes roll toward you in surprise. She is, you realize as Colin stares straight ahead with his black lenses glimmering, not the one you will miss.

The hearts are gone and there are four-leaf clovers dancing in a boozy, herky-jerky line across the windows of Keystone. After that there will be eggs and rabbits, the incongruously agrarian emblems of Easter. Then the cartoon daisies of May; the blank-windowed stretch of June ending in a barrage of patriotic iconography. It is not clear who cuts out and tapes up these things.

In the next cubicle is the nodding, unkempt head of the tall young man, who does not stop by anymore to diagnose your mental state, who just gives you tiny, perfunctory smiles in the Keystone break room, and who had a tedious conversation with you in which he admitted the night in bed was a "mistake" and that he "respects" you too much to repeat it. You hear him drone, "Because your caseworker is *busy*. Because your caseworker is not available. And if she were, she'd tell you the same thing I'm telling you right now: to take a nice, soothing bath."

Colin once said, "That's a very healthy and sane part of you: the part that gets angry when you don't get what you want."

Your switchboard blinks and shrills. You pick up.

"Get me my caseworker," a man snarls. "I need a word with that bitch."

"What is wrong?" you say.

"What's wrong is my meds. This shit's got me constipated, man. I haven't gone number two in three fuckin' days. And don't you tell me to take no bath either."

You feel the presence of Tyler behind you, the sweet drenched smell of his floral, spicy sweat. "Do you have any laxatives in the house?" you say. "Or any dried apricots? Or any coffee?"

"Yeah, I got coffee but that ain't gonna do shit. There's a fucking boulder in my gut, I'm telling you."

You explain that his caseworker can do nothing to alleviate his intestinal distress and that he will have to wait until the next business day to get the free clinic psychiatrist to adjust his medication.

"I can't wait," the man says. His voice seethes and breaks. You can feel him beginning to lose control, to abandon himself to the part of his mind that lives in a suspended and illusive state of emergency. He is giving himself over. "I need to talk to that bitch. I need her to fix this."

"She can't," you say flatly. You hear Tyler click his tongue.

"Transfer me," the man pants, "or I'm going to fucking kill myself."

The other line lights up and buzzes, and you put him on hold and pick up: "Keystone Mental Health Helpline."

It's the lady who is afraid to close her refrigerator. "Don't open it," you tell her. "Don't go near it; just hold on." Out of the corner of your eye Tyler waves his arms, and the familiar ruthlessness rears up in your abdomen: that greased track that makes leave-taking irresistible and inevitable. You switch back over.

"Hi," you say to the constipated man.

"Kill myself!" he screams.

"Look," you say, "if you feel like you're going to kill yourself, then hang up and call 911, right now."

Tyler is staring at you. The constipated man is screaming that you are a bitch and a murderous whore, and you disconnect and say to the refrigerator lady, "I'm going to tell you something about home appliances, and refrigerators in particular, and I want you to listen carefully. They're extremely strong. They're designed to weather abuse. They will not break if you open and slam them five hundred times in a row. It would be physically impossible for a human being to pull a refrigerator door off its hinges."

The woman says, "Really? I wasn't aware of that." You assure her it is the case. She pauses, and says, "That is fascinating."

Tyler is now trying to remove the phone from your hand. He is shoving "It Sounds Like You're Feeling" under your nose. The other interns silently emerge from their cubicles to witness the complete repudiation of every single helpline principle.

Next, you call 911. "Hello," you say to the operator, who has cultivated a plummy and pathologically competent tone identical to your own. You sound like two pod people conversing. You give her the constipated man's address and phone number and inform her that he has threatened suicide and is gravely constipated. She replies, "Oh, he just called us. We sent someone over there." She adds, "He does this, like, every other day."

When you stand up, Tyler is in your face, his mouth working furiously. You hear nothing. You just pick up your backpack and walk out the door into the damp leafless day. For a while you walk backward, watching the shamrocks on the windows get smaller and smaller.

You board the bus to campus with the intention of picking up a course catalogue and choosing another major. As you get off the bus you imagine a film over your body like the dusty bloom on a grape; you are dry and smooth and neutrally repellent of all things. Then you see Colin and Monty coming down the concrete steps of the Counseling Center.

You can tell what's going to happen three seconds before it does. Colin's face below the black discs is tight with concentration; he is clutching a stack of files with one hand and Monty's harness with the other, and he loses his footing; his ankles briefly intertwine mid-step before separating fiercely, frantically, as though one had burned the other. Then he falls.

You stand there. You stand and watch as Colin mutters, "Oh, dear, oh, dear," unable to voice a profanity even in distress, patting the ground with his palms, groping for his glasses which have fallen off his face, and Monty hovers over him, tail wagging, head darting.

Colin heaves himself to his feet. His glasses are on the ground, stems splayed obscenely, about six inches from your shoe. You take a step back as he pats himself with tender, distracted solicitude, checking for damage, assessing the viability of his remaining senses. He lifts his head and you see, for the first time, his naked eyes: clouded with the pearlescent, eerie radiance of cataract, unfocused, drifting, but unmistakably, almost painfully soft. You can discern no pigment. There is nothing but a colorless luster of kindness.

"Now, Monty," you hear him say. "Now, Monty. Where are they? Glasses, girl." And Monty lumbers toward you, takes the spectacles delicately in her jaws, and turns around to offer them to Colin. She is so close you could reach out and pet her.

Then they are walking away. You keep standing at the site of the fall as though the area needs to be monitored, in case other blind people come along. But you would be of no help anyway because the blind, like shamans with their animal guides and their knobby sticks, their insectlike feelers, don't need your help. Just as you used to do when you were a little kid, you put your palms over your eyes and wait to feel the difference, for the new way of seeing, the hidden way, to sink in. But all you're doing is filling in the darkness with what you already know is there: the clock tower, the concrete buildings, the grass and the trees, the person-shaped moving figures. And when you take your palms away the visual world surges toward you as if you have been missed, as if it has so many new things to show you, least among them the figures of a dog and a man—a closed circuit of brisk synchronicity, fur and flesh—moving out of your line of sight forever.

very special victims

PART I.
GOOD SAMARITAN POINTS

Her uncle told her about a rabbit named Cinnamon. It had been cute as a baby but developed extremely undesirable habits when it reached maturity. "Soon as anyone came near Cinnamon's hutch," her uncle said, twisting his mouth to one side, "he would immediately ejaculate. The whole wall was *spattered*."

Kath had the sense that he'd told this story many times to more sophisticated audiences, that it was an anecdote that went with low lights and sour-smelling drinks and that the expected reaction was laughter, but she didn't know what he was talking about, and told him so. He showed her.

"There," he said after. "Like that. *Every* time. You didn't even have to touch him."

Dr. Madden insisted Kath call her Lydia. She asked questions like, "What is your favorite subject in school?" and "Do you have a favorite stuffed animal?" and "Why don't you pretend these anatomically correct dolls are you and your uncle and show me how he touched your inchoate genitalia?" Not in those words. But she did trot out the dolls. Kath dug around in the toy box, found their clothes, and covered their starchy cloth nakedness with miniature asexual jumpsuits. Dr. Madden wrote this down.

It was tacitly understood that no charges would be pressed. Things were supposed to return to normal. But Kath knew they wouldn't. Once she finally disclosed that her mom's brother-in-law had been touching her since she was five in areas covered by a swimsuit, everything became a question of etiquette. Survival depended upon proper place settings, the micromanaged synchronization of arrivals and departures, the elusive Christmas gift that would not send a subliminally accusatory message. Her parents agonized over doorstops in the shape of mice, handcrafted by Amish people. They dithered over Precious Moments figurines. "Are you *crazy*?" Kath's father asked her mother, brandishing a little-girl Hummel clad in a perilously short pinafore and listing lederhosen. "That's *suggestive*! They'll take it the wrong way!"

Once a week, beginning at Christmas vacation, Kath's mother dropped her off at Dr. Madden's downtown office in an old grain elevator converted to a shabby-chic office space with oblong curtainless windows and chipped radiators that

clanged nonstop in the winter. It reminded Kath of the class-
rooms at St. Monica's, which were so cold that the sisters and
brothers let them wear their winter coats indoors from
Thanksgiving to Easter.

She didn't know if her parents were sending her to Dr.
Madden because she was broke and needed fixing, or because
they secretly didn't believe her and were counting on the doctor's superior interrogation methods to ferret out the truth, get
her to say she made it all up so the family could continue its
annual pilgrimages to Connecticut every Christmas to visit the
graves of its dead and sit at Aunt Amelia's gigantic festal table
without the awkwardness of carefully orchestrated seating
arrangements and a half-apologetic campaign of ostracism
against the offending uncle, Aunt Amelia's second husband.
Her parents wanted everyone to be friends. Their wholesome
holiday enclave had, at Kath's indiscretion, become tabloid
fodder.

When he wasn't scrutinizing pieces of bric-a-brac, her father
was randomly muttering things like, "I cannot believe he had
the gall. The fucking gall." Sometimes, though, Kath caught
him peering at her oddly as she watched TV or ate dessert or
roller-skated around the concrete-floored basement, caught
him staring at her as if chagrined by her unabashed engage-
ment in normal, recreational, premolestation activities. He
wanted proof. She wondered if it would be a good idea to stop
talking.

In the weeks after she told, something in her overturned, like
lifting a rock and finding the ground beneath spongy with
grubs, and she stayed up for hours bending God's ear, fetishiz-

ing prayer, clinging to His coattails and wrapping her arms around the pillars of his legs, stroking Him like a rabbit's foot rubbed to a bald knuckle. She prayed for a tornado: something annihilating and swift. She prayed to be forgiven for praying for a tornado. She thanked God profusely for letting her be born with functioning limbs. She apologized for not being nicer to her limbs and making better use of them. She prayed for a flood and for everyone to be swept away by it. And, as if in poetic justice, she wet the bed.

Christmas break felt formless, terrifying, a drifty white morass without parameters. Her parents were too embarrassed to talk to her much. She felt guilty accepting gifts from them—a board game, tiny flatware for her dollhouse, a stuffed koala, a Speak + Spell that robotically scolded her when she made an error—and kept them neatly quarantined in a corner of her room, segregated from her other toys. When she played outside, building snowmen and forts with the public-school kids from across the street, she squinted against the sun and wondered what they would say if they knew about Dr. Madden. She constantly expected to be stopped in the street, in the mall, in the grocery store, collared and made to explain herself. She counted off the days until she could return to the fluorescent-lit realm of her second-grade homeroom teacher, Sister Julia. Sister Julia was not nice. She was predictable, which was better. Squat and ruddy and choleric as the Red Queen in *Alice in Wonderland*, she addressed the class by barking out, "Gentlemen and ladies!" before making a horrible announcement about someone's illness or death—usually a priest from the rectory across the street—in tones of bitter, righteous sorrow that implied the children were to blame.

But when Kath walked into homeroom the first day after Christmas vacation, Sister Julia's iron crucifix and Reading Rainbow poster were no longer there. The room had been colonized. As if in an anthropomorphic coup, multitudes of plush teddy bears dressed in human clothing leaned against each other with drunken jauntiness all along the deep windowsills. The chalky-blue cinderblock walls were covered with posters of kittens in trees, bunnies in wicker baskets, bear cubs reading books. The very desks had broken from their row formation and arranged themselves in a circle in the center of the room. Hanging philodendrons dangled from the ceiling like booby traps.

Worst of all, Sister Julia, with her modified wimple and serge skirt and fireplug solidity, was gone. In her place was a reflexively smiling woman in red velour sweatpants and a fluffy sequin-studded sweater. Her skin was darkly tanned and leathery, her brown hair whipped into a stiffly elaborate mold, her teeth glowing white and symmetrical.

"Hi, there!" she said to every child who entered, wringing her bony hands. "Hello!"

Kath's stomach lurched. She extricated herself from the woman's shoulder-squeeze and slid into a seat beside Ali Kressler, who had been her assigned deskmate during Sister Julia's reign.

"Where's Sister?" she whispered.

Ali smoothed her uniform jumper. "That's the same bear I got for Christmas," she said, pointing to a windowsill cub in a pink acetate-and-taffeta tutu.

Kath took her pencil box out of her bookbag and waited for something resembling order to resume. Most of her classmates were gathered at the windows, manhandling bears, grabbing handfuls of Dum-Dums from ceramic candy dishes scattered here and there, under the beatific beaming of the red-velour woman. The room no longer smelled of pink erasers and drafty air. The radiators were shut off and draped in Indian tapestries. Three large space heaters, coils glowing orange, radiated blasts of arid warmth. Kath's collar itched.

Once the room was full, the strange woman hovered in front of the blackboard with her hands clasped, smiling. She made deliberate eye contact with each child in the circle, eyes sweeping the room like a high beam, while giving the impression of not really seeing any of them.

"Well, hi, there, everyone!" she said. She hopped onto Sister Julia's huge oak desk and sat cross-legged. "I bet you're all wondering where Sister Julia is!"

The class stared at her. The woman said, "Well, Sister Julia had a little family business she had to take care of, in New Hampshire. Her niece just had twins, how about that!" Her face gaped in mock astonishment. "Sister went up there to help her out for a while. So I'm going to be here working with you all for the rest of the school year. My name is Mrs. Lewis." She twisted around her torso and wrote it on the board, still cross-legged.

"Now," she continued, "Brother Andrew told me that Sister started you off with the Our Father every morning. Before I learn all your names, I thought I'd teach you *my* favorite prayer. We'll say it every day from now on."

As Kath tried to digest the mental image of Sister Julia with relatives, Sister Julia cradling twins in the crook of each stout reddish arm, Mrs. Lewis led the class in her favorite prayer:

God, grant me the serenity to accept the things I cannot change,
The courage to change the things I can,
And the wisdom to know the difference.

She made them say it three times until they memorized it.

Later, filling in blanks in her reading workbook while
Mozart played on Mrs. Lewis's record player, Kath felt her balance slowly returning, like a bobbing cork righting itself in a
current, until Ali dropped her pencil. It skittered under Kath's
feet and she picked it up and put it back on Ali's desk.

"You!" Mrs. Lewis said. She was coming toward Kath,
white teeth bared and lips drawn back with inelastic glee.
"Katherine, right?" Kath nodded. Everyone looked up.

"She's called Kath," Ali said.

"Kath, then," Mrs. Lewis said. "That was a very sweet thing
you just did! Did everyone see that, how she picked up Alison's
pencil for her? Kath, you just earned yourself a Good Samaritan
point." She strode over to the blackboard and wrote Kath's
name, with a 1 beside it. "What I want most of all is for you
to be nice to each other, to follow the Golden Rule," she said.
"Like Kath just did. Every time I see one of you doing something nice for someone else, you'll get a Good Samaritan point.
When we have a hundred points for the whole class, we'll
have a pizza party!"

The class stared at her. Then Steven Brickler raised his hand.
"What if we do something *mean* to someone else?"

Mrs. Lewis shook her chalk at him. "That's a very good
question, Steven. In that case, two points will be *deducted* from
the entire class total. So if we have ninety-eight points as a
class, but Alison hits Kath and Kath, instead of turning the

other cheek, hits her back, how many points will we have *then?*"

Ali and Kath glanced at each other guiltily, as though somehow implicated by the hypothetical scenario of violence Mrs. Lewis had conjured. Their classmates piped out figures, *Ninety-six, no, ninety-four, ninety-four, ninety-four,* none of them raising their hands, everyone tipping desks forward while Mrs. Lewis stood there beaming, nodding, waving a bouquet of red and purple and orange Dum-Dums. No one else did anything charitable and Kath's name was the only one on the chalkboard all day, singled out and numbered, like a name in a lottery or some kind of draft.

Kath had never liked the low-rent theatrics of St. Monica's lay teachers, all of whom engaged in varying degrees of starry-eyed, pandering evangelism. Every year, as the sisters and brothers got old and retired, there were more and more of them. The lay teachers started the tradition of St. Monica's annual Christmas-card photo: a still-life manger scene featuring a prepubescent Mary and Joseph and a Cabbage Patch Preemie Jesus. That December—perhaps due to the haggard, soulful listlessness that had hung over her in the weeks before disclosing her uncle's actions—Kath had been chosen as the Virgin Mary. Someone had lost the Cabbage Patch doll, and the Christ Child was portrayed by an Ewok from *Star Wars* whose dark synthetic fur protruded wildly from its swaddling clothes. Kath, cradling the hirsute Jesus, flinching as Mrs. McCollough, the music teacher, moved her into position with an intimate, sniveling gentleness that reminded her of Uncle Martin, had decided then and there that she would tell. She would put an end to it. She gazed into the lens with an expression of grim resolve that made her look less like a blessed virgin than a flinty-eyed child bride in a Walker Evans photo.

Kath thought telling would stop everything. Not just the uncle's nocturnal groping, but her own weak love for the role she played with him, the novelty persona of cosseted scamp: how she had craved and courted the attention of the uncle before his hugging and cuddling and teasing snowballed into strange, fast-breathing caresses that she could not return, that blanked her out of the scenario completely even though she was the centerpiece of it, there but not there, like the eye of a hurricane. But in the weeks before Christmas her parents had been arguing about bills and were distracted, snappish; it took a while before they realized what she was telling them and then everything escalated terrifyingly. They were both coming at her at once, necks thrust out, faces red, not blinking, their voices rising as they spat questions at her until she burst into tears with the knowledge that she had damaged everyone's life in some irreversible and unfathomable way. Afterward her mother, contrite, tried to hug her and Kath was nauseated by the soft pale flesh and the earthy smell of her mother's hair.

She grew violently averse to the queasy maneuverings of affection. She remembered the video camera, how he had followed her around with it during family get-togethers, and how she felt him feeding off her discomfort, treating her with a certain mock-tender, needling pressure, as if putting a dress on a squirming kitten. How he seemed to find her resistance adorable and, at the same time, to enjoy incrementally ratcheting up the intensity of the stimulus, patient and measured as a Chinese water-torturer, but smiling, always smiling. Looking at the videos afterward, in the family room with all the uncles and aunts and cousins, Kath could always tell when she was cognizant of his lens and when she wasn't. There were certain long-distance shots—zoomed in and in and in, jerkily—in which she didn't once look up, but she saw her own face tightening and lowering with a certain combination of noblesse oblige and frustrated shame. It was the same way she averted her attention from boys on the playground when she knew they were talking about her, when she could *hear* them but didn't want to betray her own knowledge; if she confronted it, if she let on, it would have become real. That was how she felt now, perpetually, as if the lens were a permanent part of her landscape like a spying periscope in a cartoon. She could not escape it but she could not acknowledge it either.

After the weekly meetings with Dr. Madden began and Mrs. Lewis replaced Sister Julia, Kath's overwrought prayers gave way to fantasy scenarios in which God assumed human form—hulking and male and draped in dark cloth—and hurt her physically, from afar. There was no actual touching involved: just starbursts of pain in a pristine vacuum, bright as stainless steel, and her own bottomless stoicism. She maintained perfect composure. The pain was divinely mandated. It was a force moving against her as amoral as an earthquake, and all it demanded of her was endurance. She fell asleep to fantasies of being hurt almost to death and woke up in a wet bed. Her mother always heard her get up, and came in to help change the sheets.

One afternoon Dr. Madden said, "Your mom tells me you have some problems at night, when you fall asleep."

Kath snapped to attention, wildly searching her brain for

any possible way her mother could have detected her night-
time fantasies. She felt her face grow hot and taut and was
about to deny any and all alleged perversity, when she realized
that Dr. Madden, with her customary adherence to euphemism, meant the bed-wetting.

Dr. Madden wore a midlength skirt with flesh-toned nylons,
and she crossed her legs in a careful, self-conscious way that
made Kath shiver in disgust. "Waking up in a wet bed isn't
much fun, is it?" she said. The corners of her mouth turned
down. "How would you feel if it stopped?"

"Glad," Kath said. She looked at her hands.

Dr. Madden inched forward. "How would you feel about an
alarm," she said confidentially, her face so close that Kath could
see the unblended striations of her beige foundation, "a little
alarm you could wear at night, that would wake you up as soon
as you had to go to the bathroom? How does that sound?"

Kath began to cry. She didn't mean to, and she didn't understand why soft tones of voice and direct eye contact, the wheedling seduction of these tiny kindnesses, undid her. It wasn't
sadness that brought the tears on; it was fear: the same knee-
jerk panic she felt when Mrs. Lewis began writing her little
notes on scented paper with bears on them, leaving them on
her desk, tucking them into her tests and assignments. The
notes said things like, *Kath, you look so sad. Are you all right?* and
*Kath, if you need someone to talk to, I will listen. Please know I'm
your friend.* Every time she got one, hot liquid surged to her
eyes and she had to blink several times. She threw the notes
out, in plain sight of Mrs. Lewis. She was careful to perform
no good deeds even as the others, greedy for pizza, fell all over
themselves opening doors for one another and sharing the

good parts of their lunches. Kath remained scornful, arms folded, as the tally grew and grew. What Mrs. Lewis construed as Good Samaritanism—these meaningless tokens of favor exchanged—was nothing of the sort. The Good Samaritan did not merely lubricate the gears of social interaction so that everything stayed nice on the surface and no one's pencil remained on the floor. The Good Samaritan found a half-dead person on the side of the road and took him home. Unless someone in her class followed suit, there should be no pizza. It made Kath so angry that she could barely restrain herself from snorting every time Mrs. Lewis wrote another name on the board. She fantasized constantly about telling her this, shaming her publicly.

Now Dr. Madden put a hand on her shoulder and squeezed. "It's all right," she said. "It's all right. Maybe that would be too scary, huh? You don't have to do that if you don't want to."

Kath put her hands over her face and thought of instruments of torture—*clubs, cudgels, truncheons*—words squat as fire hydrants, solid as pit bulls.

Mrs. Lewis made them form a line and handed out torn-up pieces of Wonder Bread.

"This is the Body and Blood of Christ," she said as the line snaked around the wreath of desks, "and we do not *chew* the Body and Blood of Christ. We let it dissolve in our mouths. We quietly go back to our pews, we kneel on the kneeler, and we pray, holding the host in our mouths until it is gone."

She gave each of them a shiny plastic rosary. Kath's was pink. "I picked this one out just for you," Mrs. Lewis whispered, patting Kath's shoulder and shooting her a measured, meaningful look, as if to invoke the scorned notes. Kath glanced around in horror.

After two weeks of practice, Brother Andrew, the vice principal, was brought in. "I want you to walk," he told them, "as if you have marshmallows on the bottoms of your shoes. There will be no clomping, there will be no whispering, there will be no pushing or shoving. The person sitting on the aisle"—he made a sweeping gesture—"goes first, and reenters the pew on the *opposite end* they came from. And you'll be walking like *mice*. Mice with marshmallows on the bottoms of their feet. Or I will be very upset."

Mrs. Lewis hovered in the background with arms crossed and eyes averted in mute disapproval of Brother Andrew's fear-mongering. Everyone, even the sisters, was slightly afraid of him. He reminded Kath of the granite statue of Saint Augustine, Saint Monica's son, in the school's prayer garden: immobile and upright as a chess piece, with a rippling concrete beard and a hat that looked like a bucket stuck upside down on his head. It was the same kind of hat the Pope wore for Christmas Mass on TV, but the Pope looked stooped and dwarfed by the power of the hat. On Saint Augustine it seemed to be a natural extension of his towering, terrible, corrugated forehead. He was huge. He was nine feet tall. When Mrs. Lewis took them out to the gated prayer garden to experience nature, Kath ignored Saint Francis with the Disneyfied bird on his shoulder, Saint Patrick with his staff and serpent, even the Virgin Mary, small-boned, a demure ingénue amid scowling elders, eyes downcast below her pale-blue hood. It was Saint Augustine Kath stared at, gazing up at him and knowing he was about to fall on her.

Brother Andrew had no beard and wore no hat. He wore a

long white robe with a tasseled, braided white rope around the waist, and his hamster-brown hair receded from his forehead. His anger, however, was searing and just. Last year, in reaction to plans for modernizing St. Monica's hundred-year-old cathedral, Brother Andrew had taken to the pulpit after Mass and swept his arms to encompass the marble pillars, the gigantic marble crucifix grafted onto the back wall, the wine-red velvet curtains of the confessionals, the Stations of the Cross rendered in blazing stained glass. "You can't get this at Kmart," he thundered, sweat gleaming on his balding head. "Would you *remodel* the Sistine Chapel? Would you *remodel* the Vatican?" All the children had giggled reflexively at the mention of Kmart. But Kath shivered, transfixed.

Now, ignoring the glower of Mrs. Lewis's disapproval, Brother Andrew said, "I'm not going to put up with any shenanigans, not from any one of you. I'll get tough if I have to!" Kath felt her waist disconnect from her torso. A shimmering band of numbness quivered at the place where they'd been joined.

She thought of Brother Andrew that night. She imagined a histrionic chalkboard-screech of pain on her skin: a feeling that would usurp every other, hone and flatten her into a strange, cold person of unmannered competence. She slapped her own face—softly so her parents wouldn't hear—but remained coolly unmoved. So she imagined Brother Andrew resting a warm palm on her head and saying, "I know I won't have to do this again," and the warmth of it stayed with her through the night, the unshakable sensation that he had deposited something there: an indelible residue on top of her head in the perfect shape of a hand.

In the middle of the night, she peeled off her wet pajama bottoms and underwear and remade the bed with the oiled, expressionless poise of a Kabuki dancer. Her mother didn't even wake up.

Two days before her First Communion, Kath stood in the living room as her mother fitted her for the dress she'd sewn from a Butterick pattern. It was white and lacy, with an empire waist and a long veil that hooked around Kath's ears.

"Who's doing it, do you know?" her mother asked Kath. "Is it going to be that visiting priest from Vietnam?"

"What does that matter?" her father said.

"Well, he doesn't speak English very well and I can't tell what he's saying most of the time."

"That is racist," Kath said, not accusingly, but with a certain pride in landing on the word.

"No, it isn't," her father snapped. "It's a statement of fact. I know what racism is. I took a road trip through the Jim Crow South when I was nineteen, and I *saw* racism. Don't call your own mother a racist when you don't even know what racism is."

"Will you *please*? We're trying to do something here," Kath's mother said. They began to argue in tedious circles, and her father got up and started pacing as he ranted, face red and eyebrows drawn together. Her mother kept stabbing pins into Kath's dress and Kath looked at herself in the floor-length mirror her mother had propped against the entertainment center: the veil silly atop her bowl-cut hair, the sagging knees and dirty toes of her white tights, the hole where her front teeth used to be. She took stock of the living room. Her eyes skidded over the towering oak entertainment center with its cardboard backing and its carved wooden duck and dusty encyclopedias. The murky greenish-black painting of people jumbled in a city square in the rain, wielding coppery umbrellas; the uneven black granite tiling of the foyer. Then she closed her eyes and knew that, when she opened them, she would be a different person. Things would be different. She would not be the same. It felt like she was drawing the curtains around herself.

When her eyes opened, the changes weren't visible yet and everything, including her reflection, looked the same. But she knew that things were different inside, in the parts that mattered, and that the world and everything inside of her was silently rearranging, altered by her decision to calmly, soullessly engineer an outcome.

The girls, all in white, sat in the front pew of the cathedral, the boys in the next pew dark-suited and devoid of cowlicks. Mrs. Lewis had given each of them a wrist corsage, pastel blossoms browning at the edges and cold from the fridge. Into Kath's corsage she had tucked a pink Post-it scrawled with her womanly, loop-heavy cursive: *Thinking of you today, Kath!*

The pews were scarred and smelled of lemon oil. Stuffing oozed out of the cracked red leather of the kneeler. Kath sat through the Mass needing badly to blow her nose. Then Father Nguyen was saying in his heavy accent, "This is the Lamb of God who takes away the sins of the world. Happy are those who are called to His supper." And Kath and the others murmured what they had been taught: "Lord, I am not worthy to receive you, but only say the word and I shall be healed." She hated saying this; it made her feel abased; and she muttered it through gritted teeth. Father Nguyen gave the altar boys the Eucharist. The hymn started—"Lord of the Dance" from the blue-covered missal—and the quavery old ladies dragged the pace down as usual, and Kath sang so low it was hard to discern the faint ghost of her voice droning behind all the others, tuneless but unwavering like the hum of a refrigerator, and she was briefly surprised and disturbed by how almost-dead she sounded. Then she got in line behind Ali and filed out of the pew.

Ali's veil brushed against her nose, almost making her sneeze, and she buried her face in the chilled buttery petals of her corsage. The rest was like sleepwalking. Kath had planned to furl her hands together in a bird's nest, the way they'd practiced, but at the last second, with Father Nguyen's dark eyes staring into hers benignly and his hand raised, she stuck her tongue out. As the priest said, "The Body of Christ," she answered, "Amen," with her tongue straining, lolling out of her mouth so that she felt it drying out in the air and the strong roots of it aching, and the host stuck to it: perfectly round, a primitive coin, currency of some strange and brittle country.

She couldn't remember which shoulder to touch last in the Sign of the Cross. It didn't matter. She signed sloppily and joined the procession back to the pew, chewing the host with her mouth wide open. She looked around. No one, least of all Brother Andrew or Mrs. Lewis, was paying her any attention. Kath chewed and chewed, standing up at the pew, sticking her tongue out like a cat, not kneeling at all, the host desecrated and in smithereens, and still no one turned around, no one paid witness. And it stayed that way until she gave one final grind of her teeth, assembled the small woody slivers into a sticky missile on her tongue, and spat in a glorious arc, like a cherub in a fountain, straight into the air.

Brother Andrew knew better. But Mrs. Lewis thought it was a flaw in her teachings, coupled with the indigestibility of the host: "It's not just a piece of dried-up bread, Kath," she said. "No matter what it tastes like. It's been blessed by the priest. It's *God*. It symbolizes God. I don't know if that's something that I explained well enough."

Mrs. Lewis's hands were knotted on top of Sister Julia's desk. She unfolded and wrung them, knocking over a wooden paperweight in the shape of an apple with a smiling, bespectacled worm emerging. Brother Andrew hovered behind her, arms crossed.

"She knows that," he said. "She knows." He studied Kath warily. Kath looked him in the face and wondered, from a muffled, bemused vantage point somewhere on the ceiling, what effect her large eyes were having on him. Then she blinked, thinking of God on the floor of the empty cathedral: how easily He could be mistaken for a pile of pencil shavings, debris from a pocket, a lump of sawdust. She saw the rows and rows of twinkling red votives that reminded her of pictures of Las Vegas, casting their light like watery blood on the pieces of Him, and the world going on just as before, without a blip. Everyone else had swallowed. Perhaps everyone else who ever took Christ in their mouth had swallowed. Perhaps that was enough to outweigh her transgression, to keep things functioning and pretty: the weight of all that pious bolus, all those teeth withheld. She thought of Dr. Madden, and how she now had something to tell her that would not produce a there-

there, a shoulder-pat, a flustered rummaging in the toy box, a corresponding picture book. Dr. Madden would look at her just as Mrs. Lewis was, just as Brother Andrew was: with incredulity, with something like awe. And Kath would feel as she did now: like she was sitting high up on a pyramid, like she was the very narrow and diminishing apex of something huge, at an altitude at which her bed, her eyes, her armpits could never be anything but dry.

Mrs. Lewis said, "Is that true, Kath? Did you know that? Did you understand what we've been studying, about the Eucharist?"

Kath nodded. Then she said, "Yes," and made herself laugh for Brother Andrew's benefit, because he was looking with grim assessment at his hands, as if contemplating the damage they were capable of, and how it could be tempered. "I'm going to be in my office," he said to Mrs. Lewis, "and I'd like Katherine to stop by in no less than ten minutes." He didn't look at Kath. He walked out of the room with his shoes squeaking, and they both watched his tassels dancing gracefully as he rounded the corner.

Mrs. Lewis kept staring at Kath with honest puzzlement. Kath thought she looked sort of like a monkey, the sad grizzled kind that resemble wise old gurus or ancient idiot savants. Mrs. Lewis said, "Do you want me to go with you?"

Kath shook her head.

Mrs. Lewis picked up Kath's hand, the right one with the corsage still drooping from its wrist. She plucked it from the desk like a pencil and held it in the air so long Kath was afraid she was going to kiss it. Kath's face seized. She squirmed in her seat. But Mrs. Lewis did not let go; she held Kath's hand in both of hers and she pumped it up and down, slowly, idly, almost as though she were playing a game. "I was watching you," she said, "and you didn't shake anyone's hand before Communion. You just folded your hands in your lap." Thickness rose in Kath's throat.

Mrs. Lewis moved the hand up and down several more times. Then she said, "Peace be with you."

There was a bear on the windowsill behind Mrs. Lewis's head: the only naked one in the room, Kath realized. It was not even accessorized, not even with a brooch or a tiara, and it looked cold. "What do you say back?" Mrs. Lewis said. Kath stared at the bear behind her teacher's head. She remembered this, the grand, liturgical sound of it, the seigniorial goodwill. She whispered, "And also with you."

"That's right," Mrs. Lewis said. "That's right." She let go. "I guess you can go now."

Mrs. Lewis watched her walk out, sitting in her chair with her chin cupped in one palm. Then Kath was alone in the long, shiny hallway streaked with bars of noon sunlight shifting, intersecting like crossbeams on a highway. On the walk to Brother Andrew's office she ducked under them and twisted between them, never letting them touch her just as she never walked on cracks, never took an odd number of steps, avoided the aisle seat of the pew, never ate her lunch when people were watching, never remembered which shoulder to touch last. Then, despite her efforts, a shaft of light hit her and she stopped.

She remembered a girl in her first-grade class named Rachel, a fierce blond girl who ruled the playground with the dangerous, careening charisma of a comet. One late winter afternoon as a group of them were walking home from school in the dusk, Rachel took a flashlight from her bookbag and cast a tiny stream of light, training it ahead of the group like a leashed dog with its nose to the ground, letting it test out the terrain and carve out of the dark a thin safe corridor. She said anyone who stepped out of the flashlight's path would die from lack of oxygen, that the light was all that was allowing them to breathe and the surrounding darkness was like Mars, like the moon, like a planet where the air was poison. As soon as she said it, it became true. Kath felt her lungs constrict and her heart drum out a wild SOS, and she was dying by quick degrees as the little skein of light got farther and farther away, kept moving steadily as a conveyer belt.

"Rachel!" she screamed. "Wait!"

She jostled and pushed to get into the light. She kicked and scratched. A boy named Jay, who was asthmatic, began to wheeze. Rachel relented, dousing each of them in turn with a ration of life-giving light like the priest flinging around the metal canister of incense, and all the way home they each got just enough to survive on. Then everyone procured flashlights of their own, and it became a daily ritual: a group of five or six children walking slowly home on thin tightropes of light, stooped as arthritics.

But one day, after Rachel had been expelled for putting burrs in Jennifer Jackson's hair and for some other infraction no one would talk about, Kath, walking home alone, switched off her light and found that she could breathe fine. There was no poison. She stood still for a while in the dusk, taking deep pure breaths, suffused with a strange guilty elation.

She had the same feeling now: the sensation of coming out of a spell, emerging into a world that was safer but much stranger. It weakened her and she paused to support her weight against the bulletin board of outdated New Year's resolutions. She thought she must be falling in love with herself, if such a thing was possible. There were so many soft places that had never been properly heralded: the warm silky expanse of abdomen, the inside of the wrist with its tender blue marbling of veins and its matchstick bones. She plunged a hand down her undershirt and was moved almost to tears by the chamois softness of her torso. Her fingertips dabbled in the shallow divot at the base of her throat. She thought, *This is what he liked.*

Then she remembered where she was going and what would happen. She tried to summon up the high-altitude feeling but it wouldn't come back. She feared it was gone for good, because her whole body was fizzing with the vengeful insistence of a limb awakening from sleep. Outside Brother Andrew's office she stood touching herself for so long—stroking her forearms, tracing her lips, introducing a fingertip to the heartbreaking softness of an earlobe—that he finally had to get up from his desk, put a hand on the nape of her neck, and steer her in, gently. Then he closed the door.

PART II. UNCLE

She told three men. The first stopped sleeping with her right away. Not because she was tainted or anything, he explained. It just put images in his head that were counterproductive to sustaining an erection. He felt terrible.

The second man asked a lot of questions. She didn't want to tell him—this was on the heels of the first man's reaction—but he treated her like the burial site of an ancient civilization; he dug for clues with a sweaty-palmed reverence and did not stop until he held it triumphantly aloft, that sordid tidbit like a saber tooth. He was interested in breeding. He didn't want to marry into a flawed tribe; and for months she wished herself dead and him weeping at her bedside.

The third man was different. He said it wasn't her fault. He said it had happened to him, too, although in less severe form: a random crotch-grab in a public restroom, the culprit a classic drooler in a trenchcoat with one rheumy eye. He had been fourteen and he punched the man in the face, fled the room, hid and cried and told no one. He was, he said, ashamed. He should have run to the nearest authority and turned the drooler in. The unchecked drooler could be fondling innocents at this very moment. He was so vehement on this point that she saw his terrible question coming at her like the fin of a shark, and there was no escape. "Did you ever tell the police?" he asked, and when she said no, he scolded her for being a passive accomplice to countless evil acts. "You know his name," he said. "You know his address. It's unconscionable!" He continued to ask, "Did you call the police yet?" until she refused to see him.

These were kind men. They deplored sexual deviance. The third one once said to her, "You know what I think of rape scenes in movies? It's like someone put a big, beautiful birthday cake right in front of me and took a shit on it. It's like someone shitting on my birthday cake," and she scoffed at him for trivializing the issue, but at the same time felt oddly defended and grateful.

They were all kind. But she decided to never tell another one.

———

It did not define her; the men never understood this. She did things. It was not the sum of her because she made herself do things, and the rest of the world reached a consensus that she was normal, she was competent; she was intense but in a good way. She hated Christmas and proclaimed her aversion loudly. She ran in the ravine. She was a person who ran all the time and had complicated shin issues. She refused to ever say the word *panties*, hating its simpering, cloying femininity, preferring the Sears-catalogue utilitarianism of *underwear*. She did crosswords in ink and finished nearly all of them. She read. She loved novels in which people lived in reduced-but-genteel circumstances and drank thrice-steeped tea and spoke with dispirited eloquence. She made five hundred dollars a week sharing an office the size of an elevator with two social workers, bushwhacking through the bureaucratic thicket of government grant applications and calculating how many Units of Service were contained in each sandwich, condom, and pair of socks disbursed; she cared about social injustice, and, true to her Catholic-fusion upbringing—both Franciscan and Jesuit orders were strongly represented on both sides of the family tree—she committed herself equally to intellectualism and altruism. Meaning she was soft enough to empathize with the plight of the poor but shrewd enough to analyze and parse them for maximum financial return. Still she was secretly a little afraid of the homeless people she raised money for. Not afraid that they would harm her, but that they would haunt her, take up tenancy in her mind and heart and crowd out the things that kept her functioning.

She had enough to worry about already—for example, the

insistent demands of the third man. She couldn't help thinking of them, because he kept calling to reiterate.

"Just tell me his name," he said over the phone. "Just a first name is all I need. I'll do the rest."

"The rest?" she said. She was stirring sauce on the stove.

"The rest," he said.

She switched off the heat and visualized the third man's lips close to the receiver and moving emphatically, like a cinematic tight shot of a villain demanding ransom. "If you're thinking of the police," she said, "it's pointless. First of all, the police are not my friends. Second, we're talking about twenty years ago. I was in grade school. There's a statue of limitations."

"Statute," the third man said. She hated it when he corrected her. "And that doesn't matter. Whether he's actually arrested or not doesn't matter. The thing is to let him know it's not okay. To let him know he's being watched. It's a deterrent."

She remembered how the third man had once turned to her while she was reading and said in a voice flat with impersonal awe, "Your face is beautiful." He said it as if her beauty were the beauty of a dead thing, a butterfly framed and dried; it could do neither of them any good.

She said, "He isn't even around any little girls anyway." She kept stirring because she didn't know what else to do. "I was the only niece. He has no daughter, no granddaughter. He's not like your guy. He's not a roving weirdo running all over town." Her voice roughened.

They argued some more and she hung up, then poured her sauce over cooled pasta and vegetables and sat down to eat. She wondered why she was able to eat after this conversation, and if it meant something was wrong with her. Coiling the noodles around her fork was strangely absorbing. She became lost in the round green integrity of a single pea, cupping her attention around it like hands, and when she disengaged herself she realized her dinner was cold and the dining room window was dark.

She put her fork down and sat back. The people across the courtyard were celebrating a birthday. Their lives seemed constructed of smartly colored geometric shapes. Through a bright square of window she saw a woman walking like a bride while carrying a blazing wheel of cake. The man she was walking toward was grinning, receptive, saving up breath for his big part, and when she placed the frosted circle in front of him he reared his head back, dragonlike, and extinguished all its light.

A month later, her lease ended and she did not renew it. She moved to a new apartment in a half-gentrified part of town that smelled of hops and oatmeal from the nearby breweries and Pillsbury plants. There were train tracks everywhere. Children dangled off corroded jungle gyms. The neighborhood had the carved-out, makeshift feel of a hobo camp and she found it oddly soothing, the shambling lullaby of the trains at night, their click click click hypnotically monotonous as a skipping record, the starchy soup of fog in the morning. She biked north to work every day past an abandoned casket factory, rows of moldy Victorians, morning glories entangled in fences and opening their blowfish mouths in the light.

She told herself she had moved to be closer to work. The People's Right to Live drop-in was ten blocks from her new place. But the move was partly for the benefit of the third man. She enjoyed imagining him learning about her relocation secondhand and marveling at the cold resourcefulness it took to orchestrate an entire move without telling a soul or asking for help.

For a while she felt safe. But her new place—a big shotgun flat in a converted rooming house, with spiky stucco walls and bad wiring—was uneasily silent. No matter how often she made tea and how invitingly she decorated her bed, she was plagued by waves of heartsick edginess, like a passenger who'd waited hours for a train only to realize that she'd been in the wrong depot all along: a sickly, hollow dawning. She ran more than ever. In her dreams she kept missing crucial appointments by a slim margin of time, and woke each day with a sore jaw from grinding her teeth. She waited for the third man to find her, or at least send an emissary. But no one called.

When the phone finally rang, it was her mother.

"Do you still want those dishes?" her mother said.

She began to cry. As always during displays of emotion, a specter hovered in the cool lobby of her brain, waiting for the signal to step in and put a stop to it.

"Oh, honey," her mother said. "What can I do? Don't you like your new apartment? You were so excited about it."

She swallowed air and said, "It's dirty. It's so dirty here, I've cleaned and cleaned and I'm not the one who made it this way, you know I'm not a slovenly person, I don't live in squalor—"

"I know that, honey," her mother said. "You're a very clean person. Remember how you used to vacuum the whole house when you came home from school, before I got home from work? I remember how nice it was to come home to a freshly vacuumed house. Remember how mad you'd get when Dad would step all over the carpet with his shoes on and ruin your beautiful vacuuming job? You did such a good job."

She laughed weakly. "I was a weirdo," she said.

"No," her mother said adamantly. "You were a good person and a helpful person. And you still are. You're always helping people. You help people no one else cares about!"

"I cared so much about the vacuum," she said, and began to cry anew. The image of herself in the house where she grew up, making back-and-forth furrows like a plow horse, made her feel horribly vulnerable. She knew she was being self-indulgent, but she didn't want the ghostly bouncer to step in yet.

"Why don't I come over?" her mother said. "I'm going to stop by and we'll clean the place together. You just need some help, honey. You just need help."

"I do," she said. "I do."

The mother waited until after a great deal of cleaning had been done—the blinds taken off the windows and soaked in the bathtub, the baseboards scrubbed, the ceiling fans dusted, and the linoleum doused in bleach—before telling her about the uncle.

"What I was told," she said, wiping her forehead carefully, "is that he got religion."

The daughter looked out the living room window, toward the casket factory and the Grain Belt brewery. The air smelled of refrigerator and leavening. "What religion?" she said.

The mother looked down at the gleaming baseboards. "I

don't know, that doesn't ever mean a particular creed, does it? 'Got religion'? It's sort of like a generic born-again thing, I guess. Definitely not Catholic, but then he wasn't born one. And he never officially converted for Amelia." She picked up a dirty sponge and tossed it aside. "All I know is, he's going to these churchy meetings and he's taking it very seriously. That's what Amelia says. She's not very happy about it."

The stucco wall looked like white meringue stiffly whipped into peaks. She sometimes felt the urge to put her tongue to it.

"I'm telling you this," her mother said, "because I think . . . because of his religious calling or whatever . . . that he might contact you. He might seek you out."

The daughter laughed. "Seek me out?"

Her mother laughed, too, flailing one wrist in a minimizing gesture, loose with uncoordinated relief and anxiety. "I don't know. There's some emphasis on making amends. They talk in these strange pilgrimage terms. So Amelia says."

The daughter said, "So Aunt Amelia told you this. Aunt Amelia said, 'My husband is going to seek out your daughter and apologize for what he did.' As plain as that?"

"Well. Not exactly as plain as that."

She turned just enough to see her mother's profile. "How much does she know?"

"If anyone told her," the mother said, "it was him."

They sat in silence for a while. Her mother kept glancing sideways at her with anticlimactic intakes of breath, as if about to speak. Then she blurted out, "You know what I never could understand? How you always wanted to be with him!" Her eyes stretched wide. "I thought, *The kid* wants *to be around him, what could he possibly be* doing *to her that's so bad?* I mean, he wasn't the type of man you'd think would— My sister wouldn't have married him if she thought he was. Would she?"

The daughter had once called her mother a bad mother and made her cry. She didn't want to do it again.

She said, "How do they even know where I live?"

Her mother flicked a foot up and down and did not answer right away. Then she said, "Amelia asked for your new address a while ago. I didn't really think twice; what was I supposed to say? It was before I ever dreamed she knew . . . you know, anything about it."

In the silence the ceiling fan rollicked around and around, its unsteady revolutions weirdly comic. It seemed to be winding up for a dramatic liftoff and the daughter almost laughed. Then a thin peevish misery, runny as yolk, spread over her. It was all very banal. The sun was boring, bland with midday virtue; there were ants on the floor and the clicking of the trains was depressingly productive and brisk. She had a sense that this encounter was not what it should be. Things should feel sharper in general right now, and less like cardboard. Life should seem much less ridiculous, more urgent than it did when her mother finally looked her in the face, not reaching out but backing away now, each breath between words a frantic hand-flap, a shooing away: "I always wanted to know, honey, what *was* it? What could it have been? When you kept being around him. When you just kept coming back!"

The daughter wanted to say, "I didn't."

But she had. She had gone back again and again: to pretend to understand his stories and laugh at what was supposed to be funny and to be lifted like a sack, with an affectionate casualness that proved her lightness, her doll-like simplicity, the reassuring physicality of someone else's entitlement to her. She had never since been borne into the air with so little ceremony.

What she said was, "Shut up." She imagined her own eyes pale and lizardlike, looking at the mother. "Will you shut the fuck up?" she said, her voice louder this time. The mother looked out the window.

Over the next few weeks she couldn't keep her hands off herself. At work she was competent, composing government grants with the whimsical earnestness of the postgraduate. Her coworkers were wary, unshockable women in their mid-thirties and indignant, aging gay men; they all liked her and indulged the precocious sass that emerged after her trial period of anxious sweetness ended. Gainful employment was still a dress-up game, one she was good at. Lately, though, she found herself looking forward to returning home as soon as possible in order to devote her full attention to masturbating until she cried. It was something she needed, in the artless prodding way of a food craving.

It was the only thing that made sense: to go to her unmade bed and bring herself off over and over, not languorously, not ardently, but like a rat pressing a lever. Once in a while she felt a tiny stun-gun of clarity right after she came. In these moments she would regard her hands with a sober appreciation for their perfection and dexterity. The sensitivity of their little hairs. Their cunning joints. Then she would start sobbing.

She had learned to make herself come by the time she was

four and had never been ashamed of it, but her orgasmic aptitude now felt tainted with a question she realized had always
been there, uneasy and lurking: Which came first, the pervert
or the egg? She shuddered to think that the furious, murky
attentions of the uncle were the unspoken consequence of her
precocity, like blindness and hairy palms. Or were they the
impetus? It was intolerable to remember her child self, small,
exultant, striving on her twin bed like a salmon going upstream,
humping toward the end point where she knew the feeling
would surge and surge and then subside. It was intolerable to
entertain the possibility that the whole dizzying ceremony,
that strange solemn elation she had guarded and held to her,
was nothing but a conditioned response. And so she did it
again and again as though she had something to prove by it.
She clubbed herself dumb with it until one day she couldn't.

It was a Saturday morning. She sat back against the headboard and assessed her surroundings with the grim, bloodshot
closure of a drunk coming out of a bender. Her options fanned
out cryptic as tea leaves. She called the third man.

"What the hell?" he said. "I've been trying to call you for
weeks."

"My number changed. I moved."

He asked where and she described the trains and the facto-
ries and the bread smell. She made him laugh once or twice.
Then there was silence and he said, voice dipping in a nakedly
aggrieved way that made her feel scarily womanly and remiss,
"Well, why are you calling me now? Since you didn't even
bother to mention you were moving."

She stood up, put a hand between her legs, and was bemused
by the leaping, responsive pulse of herself: some gamely wag-

ging trouper under the rubbed-raw skin. Her body was a perplexed animal, ever ready to serve. It forgave everyone everything.

She said to the third man, "I have something you want."

"What?" he said, wary; she was never one to be coy about sexual matters.

She said, "A name."

His face had lost its customary zealotry. Stripped of it, he seemed washed-out and sheepish: the mild-mannered alter ego of his former self. He wore a puffy coat she did not recognize.

"Is it really cold enough for that?" she said.

He caught the screen door with his elbow and shuffled into the kitchen. "I rode my bike," he said. "The wind."

She stuck a tea bag in a cup of boiled water and told him to sit down in the living room; he did, sticking his hands between his thighs to warm them: an uncharacteristic and studied gesture.

He took the cup she offered and said, "How's the People's Right to Life?"

"Right to Live," she said. "The other day this client got cited for having an unlicensed dog. It's fucking ridiculous. That dog's a registered service animal. Now she has to give it up or lose her SSI."

"Acronyms," he said.

"Oh. Supplemental Security Income." She swallowed. "And in the meantime there are flashers all over the ravine, showing off their dicks to kids on picnics, and the police think it's a better use of their time to steal some homeless lady's dog with AIDS." She paused archly. "Excuse me. Acquired Immune Deficiency Syndrome."

"The dog has AIDS?" He sipped.

"The lady." She had the sensation that someone who knew her well, a sister if she had one or a close high school friend, was watching this exchange from above and snorting in disgust at both of them.

The third man eased himself off the couch and sat on a floor pillow with his knees up. "This apartment's weird. Your other place was nicer."

"This is cheaper."

"It really does smell like beer outside."

"Yeah, well, it could smell like something worse."

The third man pressed his lips together and eyed the cracked plaster of the living room wall. "So," he said. "What's his name?"

"Guess." She deliberately flattened her voice so it would sound deadpan, contemptuous, less like some flirtatiously sassy challenge.

He shrugged. "I don't know. Larry?"

She shook her head.

"Bert?"

"No one is actually named that."

"Yes, they are," he said. "I've known people named Bert."

She looked at him and had the urge to go running, right then, in the ravine, past the rained-on mattresses and trembling footbridge, the graffitied rocks and the flashers, bouncing complicit glances off the other runners as her rib cage lifted and lowered.

"That's enough for you to go on," she said. "It's not Larry, and it's not one of the many Berts you've supposedly come across in your time. You can narrow it down from there."

She expected a scene. But he just shrugged. "Well, that's helpful. That was worth the bike ride."

She snorted. "Do you think I just wanted an excuse to lure you over here?" She thought, *What an inane encounter,* over and over.

He stood up and dusted off his pants for no reason. "No! I was glad to come. I've been worried. I just wanted to see if you were doing okay, I guess."

She stared at him. She had the sensation she was shrinking. "Okay?" she said.

He nodded.

"What about the police? What about me having a responsibility to . . ." She trailed off.

The third man shrugged again. "I think I was kind of infantilizing you. You know? It's up to you to come to terms with this thing how you see fit, is what I mean. It's not my business." He spoke without looking at her, and fidgeted with the zipper of his coat.

She had never hated him before; she did now. She scrutinized him for a trace of the taut, hunted shiftiness men's faces assumed when they were driven to be with her and didn't know why. It was never sweet. They were never besotted, just stiffly, sullenly advancing as though shoved toward her from behind. Sometimes they looked at her like an animal eyeing an untrustworthy trainer; other times in a gauging, measuring way, like she was an obstruction they needed to lift and move to get what they wanted.

And although there was nothing of this in the third man's

face, although he just stood there in her living room looking gamely uncomfortable, she came forward and pressed her palm against his crotch. She looked down at it. And when he put his hands on her shoulders and said, "What are you doing?" she fumbled with her belt buckle, heard its gratifyingly heavy clink, began to unzip.

Her breathing was perfectly even, as though she had been granted a surgeon's access to her own insides, lifting and lowering her rib cage tenderly with both hands and guiding banners of breath in and out of her throat like a fire-eater. For a few seconds she knew the shamanesque power of them all: the man in the bathroom, the flashers in the ravine, the uncle with his wormy silk-sweater smell and his aura of raspy restless movement like a cricket's legs scraping, the ease with which he reached into himself and split the seam demarcating what he did from what he was. Then got up the next day and ate cereal. Petted dogs. Engaged in the poignantly vain grooming rituals of a middle-aged man: the inspection of gums, the sculpting of sideburns.

The third man peeled her hand off and said, "I'm not doing this with you." He sounded resigned yet rehearsed, as though he'd glumly anticipated having to say this.

She stepped back, breathing hard and furious. "Oh, because I'm not allowed to have a sex drive," she said. "Every time you get a hard-on, is it because a pervert grabbed your dick in a bathroom?"

Looping his backpack over one shoulder, he was walking toward the door now. When he reached the big double-oven he backed against it and looked down at her and said, "You don't get it. What happened to me wasn't that serious."

"Can't quantify it," she singsonged, wagging a finger. This was paraphrased from *Wounded Partners in Healing*, which they'd read together.

He just kept talking. "What happened to you was, though. It was really bad. I don't think you even realize that. And I am not going to sleep with you. You need to figure your shit out on your own time. Under your own jurisdiction. Or it won't count."

"You're like a shitty fortune cookie."

He shrugged. She didn't remember him being such an inveterate shrugger. He had always been too incapable of concession to shrug even in casual conversation.

"I'm sorry," he said. Then he opened the door.

She stood on the back porch and watched him cross the yard, his back sloped like a mountain climber's, a carriage both braced and slouchy. He swung one leg over his bike. She thought of his meditative, bittersweet ride home to his normal-smelling neighborhood, a sage's flinty smugness in his eyes, the wind in his righteous hair. She thought of several things she could yell after him. But all that came out was something she hadn't known was on the tip of her tongue: the uncle's real name, over and over. Not yelled but simply thought, and long after he rode away.

There were three men and that was all. The third was the last one she told.

Eventually she saw other men, and kept her mouth shut through Oscar-winning movies in which innocents were diddled; through endless televised parades of Very Special Victims; through the initial ten seconds of sex that were always fraught

with panic, her heart whinnying, pawing, walleyed. She gen-
tled it down and kept moving. She did things, tending her
body with the disinterested briskness of a nurse.

About six months after the third man's visit, she was running in the ravine when a man stumbled out of the underbrush
with his pants around his ankles. She stopped and looked at
him. Birds chirped. The air around her seemed to soften, deli-
quesce with sweet rot. A mother duck and three ducklings
glided through the Mississippi. The man had freckled thighs
and was knocked-kneed. His eyes, deep-set and brown as the
river, met hers and he flushed, looked back and forth, and suddenly covered himself—not shamefully, but with a whiplash
grab of self-preserving instinct. Then he turned about-face and
blundered back through the brush, clutching at the waistband
of his khakis.

He seemed less of an exhibitionist than an apparition, some
feral creature separated from his tribe. She pictured more of
them back there, hunkering fearfully and waiting for her footsteps to fade. She imagined what otherworldly powers they
superstitiously ascribed to her by firelight, how they warned
their young and disbanded camp at the scent of her. The next
day she said to a coworker, "Some naked guy popped in front
of me in the ravine, but soon as he saw me he looked all horrified and ran away. I didn't know flashers were so discriminat-
ing." The coworker, one of the gay men with whom she
pored over celebrity gossip magazines in the lunchroom, said
the flasher likely wasn't a flasher at all and that the ravine was
notorious for illicit gay-sex trysts; didn't she know that? She
shrugged. She was inexplicably disappointed.

The next day the uncle came.

She was at the kitchen sink, doing dishes in the pastel wash of the setting sun, and when she heard his footsteps she looked out the screen door and her mind went blank. Somewhere in her brain, she had mislaid his significance. His face, bobbing up the back porch stairs, was blandly ubiquitous as a television personality's. But then he said her name. Conventional wisdom claimed smell as the beeline to memory, but for her it was the sound of her own name on someone's tongue: a calling card coded with sensory nuance, redolent of the nature of their claim on her and their preferred method of collection. He rapped on the screen door, and it never occurred to her not to let him in.

The uncle made a fussy show of scraping his shoes on the doormat. He looked the same. She hadn't seen him in five years, having evaded family reunions and holiday galas since the age of eighteen.

"May I come in?" he said, although he was already.

"Yeah," she said. She flapped an arm toward the dining table. She didn't know what to say next, so she said, "Want some water?"

"No, no, no; no trouble on my account, please." There was a charged subtext to this, employed like a flexed muscle.

She leaned against the sink. He stood by the refrigerator with his hands at his sides. "My mother said you might come," she said.

"Yes," he said. He kept looking at her searchingly. He wore a good-quality coat, beige and belted tightly. His hair was slightly grayer and his eyes were still round and harmless-looking, with jaunty little eyebrows like a dog's vestigial markings. He didn't smell the same, though. There had been an acidic sharpness. It was gone.

The uncle cleared his throat. "So I've been trying to start a clean slate with my life," he said. "Your mom may have mentioned it." He waited. She said nothing. He went on, "Part of that is trying to make things right with those I've wronged. And I know it must be upsetting for you to see me. And I wrestled with this, you have no idea; I asked myself, is it selfish to dredge this up? Do I have any right? And maybe I don't. Maybe I don't. But this is not about reducing karmic debt; please understand that. This is not something to cross off a to-do list. This," he said, inhaling as if about to plunge underwater, "is the central black hole of my life."

She sneezed violently. "Excuse me."

"Bless you," he blurted. He seemed grateful for the opportunity to bestow this benediction.

"Look," she said, tucking her hair behind her ears, "this really isn't necessary."

"I think it is."

"Well," she said. "Maybe for you it is. If this is a big thing for you, say what you need to say. Go for it."

"I appreciate it," he said. His constant head-bobbing and knee-jerk deference made her feel like a guru in a kung-fu movie, attended by a bowing, scraping apprentice. She smiled coldly. She articulated the action to herself as she performed it: *I am smiling coldly.*

"I don't want to just make a speech at you," the uncle said. "I was hoping we could have kind of a give and take." His voice tilted up. She recognized it, that cocksure wheedling.

"I don't think so," she said.

The uncle's round eyes began to fill up, taking on the hazy mirage-like illusion of movement that preceded full-fledged weeping. Then he blinked the water away. "All right," he said. He looked down at his galoshes. She remembered how his vacated shoes and his socked feet used to give off an earthy, pungent odor, not unpleasant, the expansive warm smell of something tightly contained and suddenly freed.

"I just want to say one thing," he said. He extended an arm as though tempted to grab her for emphasis, but quickly withdrew it. "What I did," he said, "was not your fault. I know . . . I've read the literature. I know a lot of people grow up thinking there's something wrong with them. That they're to blame. And they are not. It was me, it was all . . . my sickness. It could have been anyone. You were there, and you were—accessible. That was it. That was *it*." He made a slicing gesture, then winced at his own immoderation.

She pictured him reading the literature. She had read it, too. Then she said, "I'd feel better if it did have something to do with me. Is that sick?" The uncle took a breath to speak and stopped short. He was at a loss.

He opened and closed his mouth. He took a step forward and back again. Then he did a strange thing: he bowed his head and covered his eyes with his hand.

She leaned against the stove and watched him for a while, earnestly but without investment, the way children watch parades and inaugurations and tedious civic rituals in general. The uncle's fingers dug hard into his temple.

The niece thought of self-defense. She thought of calling the police, much as she hated them. She wondered if this was a dangerous situation; technically, there was a lawbreaker and a deviant in her home. But she could see that something in him had shut against her. She was an emblem he distorted at will, a monster disarmed. He had to turn her into something else. And for a moment she felt that he had succeeded: her hands were folded in front of her, her chin pointed down, and she thought she must resemble an old daguerreotype she saw long ago in a textbook, a pioneer woman on a prairie: salt of the earth and grimly unsexed, frozen in the eternal posture of one who bears up, bears up, bears up, then dies.

The uncle was now sitting on a wooden chair as though a giant hand had dropped him there by the scruff of the neck. He rubbed his forehead with thumb and fingers. His flesh pleated and reddened. He was right there in front of her. She thought of him having sex with his wife. She stared at his hands. They were small hands, chapped and pinkish, with spatulate fingers and broad nails, and the first time they touched her—the back of the neck, brushing—she had not been afraid.

She had never been afraid of him. What she felt now, what she had always felt, was collusion: uneasy, dead-eyed, and leaden. It began in the back of the throat and slowly sifted downward, dragging heaviness to her base like a punching bag with a weighted bottom, rooting her to the ground with the knowledge that she belonged in this kitchen with this man, that she was born here and would die here and that there was no other scenario in which she would ever be so wholly herself.

She coughed and the uncle looked up. He looked at the corner of the wall where two cupboards met.

"I told Amelia about us," he said.

She looked at him sharply. For the first time since his arrival, her interest was piqued. "She forgave you?"

The uncle shook his head. He wasn't pleading now. He was just looking at her sanely and tiredly. He was trying to get through to a tiresome woman. "Honestly," he said, "I'm not sure if she even believed me."

The niece snorted: an instinctive response. She caught the scent of incipient melodrama in her nostrils like seeping gas, and it terrified her.

She suddenly couldn't stop talking.

"Really," she said, "it's not really something I think about on a daily basis. I mean, do you just sit around thinking about it all the time? Because that's almost as creepy as having done it in the first place." She laughed. "Isn't it?"

"It was my vagueness that made her not believe me," the uncle said sadly. "I need to name it. No more euphemism. We need to stop referring to what happened as 'it.' I need to stand up and say what we did in concrete terms. To her. And to you. And to myself."

She could think of nothing worse. She knew she couldn't let this happen. She was moving toward him now and the walls of the kitchen seemed to narrow around them as she came closer, feeling taller and wider, her shadow throwing darkness over him like a tarp.

"What are you doing?" the uncle said.

She stepped forward. She knew she had to stop him but she couldn't think of anything else to say. So she just stared at the uncle's unremarkable face as if she could freeze it there, and after a few moments of staring she found it, the look she'd searched for in the third man: the taking-over and the leaving-behind. The bullish emptiness of the eyes. It was there. Then it wasn't; his face seemed to skip a frame and he was turning around, the uncle, he was clutching at his collar with one hand, he was moving toward the door.

"I'll go," he said, not looking at her. "I'll just go. I'm sorry."

He did not sound sorry. He threw the words like baking soda on a grease fire. He was another chastened, decent man who closed the door without slamming it and walked through the rain to his sad car. It was so stupid it was criminal. The car revved up and crunched over gravel.

The kitchen grew chilly. As darkness set in she wrapped her arms around her torso. She continued to stand there like that, because it was cold, because she could hear the train's skip, skip, like a bad heartbeat, and she knew the morning glories were closing their throats for the night, and because it was hard, in that clenched fist of twilight, to think of anything other than the men she had told, and what they had said to her. Things like, *Some of the sex stuff, it's not healthy.* And, *I am so so so sorry.* And, *Get over here.* And, *Nothing will ever hurt you again.* And, *Why did you let him?* And, *I can't.* And, *What can I do?* And, *This is repetitive.* And, *Somewhere in the world people are starving.* And, *You have to tell me what feels good.* And, *I want to feel your clit on my tongue. Please, for me.* What was the point of it all, this exhaustive cycle of call-and-response, disclosure and reaction? She thought with relief of the fourth, fifth, sixth, and seventh men, from whom she would never hear a word on the subject.

She heard sirens in the distance, wailing and persecutory, in hot pursuit of someone. She wondered who was being chased. Her first thought was of the uncle, but that couldn't be: Who would have told, and why would they care? The one they should be chasing, she thought, was her. She imagined herself lying on pavement, the blue-uniformed silhouettes of men looming over her. How grateful she would be as she waited for them to deliver their most merciful line, that rote benediction bestowed on every single person in trouble: the insane and the reasonable, homeless and naked, innocent and guilty, uncles and nieces. *You have the right to remain silent.*

look, ma, i'm breathing

After it was over, it seemed silly to say she'd been in danger. The man hadn't hurt her or even threatened to. Isabel made a living out of transforming the molehills of her life into mountains. There was her memoir, after all, which buffed a single childhood gaffe to a high shine of profound tragedy. It garnered the usual overheated blurbs—*relentless*; *brave*; *an indictment of religion's hypocrisy as well as her own*; *at its essence, profoundly forgiving*. Without it, the man would have lacked ammunition. And after the whole ordeal was over, after her friends had stopped calling to make sure she was all right, after she'd stopped reading the courthouse papers, she sat in her living room and stared at her name on the spine of the book and wondered if she had the right to feel traumatized at all, or if she, like any wunderkind facing a sophomore slump, was merely courting a sequel.

It was true: she had wanted the apartment, had tried hard to look legitimate and solvent. When she wrote *Writer/Teacher* as her occupation on her rental application, she noted in parentheses the name of the famous school where she taught, the school she never would have gotten into as a student and whose campus she still sometimes got lost on after six months as an associate professor of English, as she wandered across identical quad upon quad. She wrote down her faculty Web page in case the landlord thought she looked too young to hold such a position. And under "personal references," she cited the best-known of her colleagues: a political theorist who made forays into satirical fiction. People recognized his name as noteworthy even if they couldn't remember why. She made sure to capitalize the proper letters in *Ph.D.*

The landlord hadn't seemed impressed. There was something off about him: his stoicism bordered on blankness. He appeared to be gazing determinedly through a blind spot. But now and then he seemed to catch a glimpse of whatever lay beyond it, and a sudden flash of feeling would kindle in his eyes, as if he were being shown some internal reel of images that did not quite cohere. He was a lanky man in his early fifties. His hair was still dark and plentiful. He wore a tool belt around his waist.

"There's three nice big closets," he said. "One's probably big enough to be a small study, if you don't mind not having any windows while you work."

"Well," Isabel said, smiling, "I can write anywhere."

He was holding a hammer. He put it down on the kitchen counter and showed her around—the newly tiled kitchen with its dishwasher, the bricked patio surrounded by cedar fencing, the washer and dryer hidden in a cunning little storage shed, the redone bathroom. He narrated the tour with an account of all the repairs he'd made, how he practically had to gut the place, redo the wiring, renovate down to the studs. He wanted to preserve its historical integrity. Pointed out his choice of octagonal black-and-white tiles for the bathroom: "Authentic," he said, "just like the nineteenth century." Described how he scraped dingy paint from the scalloped wainscoting, inch by inch. He told her all this in an almost perfunctory way, but with a slight air of irritation, as if there were something combustible, propulsive, underneath. She would come to recognize this as typical. He spoke as if he expected every topic to erupt into an angry debate for which he was amply armed.

"My great-aunt—my wife's aunt, actually—owns this place, the whole building," he said. "She lives in the flat upstairs. This downstairs apartment has been vacant for years. I retired last year and started really working on sprucing up these family properties."

"Well," Isabel said, "you've done a beautiful job with the renovation. Everything looks just spectacular."

"Thank you," he said. He smiled for the first time. The smile was a surprise: it transformed the cragginess of his face, making him look boyishly grateful.

Encouraged, Isabel started babbling, demonstrating a girlish enthusiasm that fit her poorly, even though it was genuine— she *did* love the place, she wanted to live there, but she never felt so insincere as when gushing over something she was honestly excited about.

The landlord seemed to appreciate the effort that went into her litany of embellishments, a wish list of domestic accoutrements worthy of *Queen for a Day*: how great it would be to have a washer/dryer, no longer to have to lug her laundry through the filthy streets of her sketchy neighborhood; how she'd been longing for a nice big claw-foot bathtub instead of her tiny three-cornered shower with its trickly water pressure; and the patio!—how wonderful to have an outdoor space where she could finally grow herbs, annuals, and perennials, all the graceful California flora flourishing in twisty-limbed pro-fusion, so different from the austere and sooty foliage of the Midwest. It was Little Match Girl territory: the stuff of her memoir.

"I'll tell you what," the landlord said. "There was a woman to see the place earlier this morning, had a baby with her, and she might be coming back with her husband any minute. So I don't know. What you gotta understand"—and he loomed close, Isabel forcing herself to meet his dark eyes, because she didn't want to seem shifty—"is that the decision is my aunt's, not mine. Since she owns the place. But you're welcome to step out on the deck and finish the application, and I'll see what I can do."

Isabel let him lead her outside. She sat down on a patio chair and finished her application, rooting in her bookbag for her credit score and her current landlord's number. She wrote carefully in a penmanship that did not come naturally to her: exaggeratedly rounded, almost childish, each letter unmistak-able as the oversized examples in an alphabet primer. It took her about ten minutes. She looked around the yard, admiring its twining nasturtiums and rosebushes. Then she opened the French doors of the patio and stepped inside to find that the previously empty kitchen was now full of strangers.

The landlord stood there with a young couple: a pretty woman whose saucer-eyed infant dabbled its fingers in her broom-colored ponytail, and her husband, a hipsterish and artfully tousled young professional. The man and the woman oozed the kind of sheepish magnanimity that comes from securing the exact outcome they had strained, hurried, and cajoled to get. Next to them sat an elderly woman on a kitchen stool. She was gazing at the baby.

Isabel stood in the middle of the kitchen with her application. The landlord saw her there and his face tightened with one of its brief, pained spasms of feeling.

"Isabel," he jumped in, gesturing toward the old woman, "this is my great-aunt, Marjorie. She's ninety-two years old."

The old woman whinnied out a shocked laugh. "Now, why on earth did you tell her that?"

The young mother piped in, "It's because you look so much younger!" She grinned at the landlord for support. He just kept looking at his aunt. Then he hustled Isabel into the living room as the couple fussed over their checkbook and the lease agreement.

"Look," he said, lowering his voice, "if my aunt hadn't happened to show up when those people came back in, you would've gotten the place. But she likes the idea of renting to a family."

"Oh, I understand," Isabel said. She briefly shimmered with resentment of the family in the next room—their shameless kowtowing, dangling that baby in the old woman's face.

The landlord was still talking. "I would've let you have it for one simple reason," he said. He spoke low and flat and close to her ear, but without looking at her, as if they were

Secret Service agents. "You're smarter than them. And I'd rather rent to smart people. They're easier to reason with, in my experience."

"Oh," Isabel said.

Later she wondered why this comment hadn't raised a red flag. But at the time, as she and the landlord stood together in this oddly conspiratorial posture, all she could think about was how badly she wanted the place. Wanted the bucolic mystique of this neighborhood with its bald hill, its water tower, its hidden, snaking staircases and communal gardens, its tumbledown beachy cottages. Wanted to begin some hazy, pastel phase of living: not a life so much as a restful afterlife, compared to what had passed earlier.

Then the landlord said, "Listen here. Tell me how this sounds to you."

He explained that he had another family-owned property, less than three blocks away, in the same neighborhood. A turn-of-the-century little white dormered house with a picket fence, backyard with an avocado tree and rosebushes and fuchsia, big country kitchen, wainscoting and pocket doors and wood floors and window seats and stained glass.

"Meet me there tomorrow morning," he said, "and I'll show you around. I haven't listed the place yet, but I'm renting it more than sixty percent under market value, as long as I can get a tenant in there I trust. I go on instinct. I go on gut. And I have a good feeling about you."

When she saw the house the next morning, her first thought was, *This isn't fair.*

Nothing about it was fair. Not the white clapboard siding,

dilapidated and weathered in all the right places, not the over-grown rosebushes, high on the crest of a hill. Not the gabled windows. Not the front door's heart-shaped keyhole. Isabel waved and smiled when the landlord appeared, emerging from a basement entrance holding a rusty toolbox.

"This is beautiful," she burst out.

The landlord gave one of his rare, satisfied smiles, and said, "Thought you'd like it."

He seemed excited, less inhibited than the day before. He kept up a running commentary as he led her into the rustic, slate-tiled kitchen.

"Check this out," he said, indicating the cabinetry. "After the '89 earthquake, I went down and salvaged these drawers from what was left of the old court building. See, they still have case names on them."

Indeed, the drawers were affixed with tiny metal frames encasing old, laminated file names in sepia ink.

"That is awesome," Isabel said. "A little piece of history."

"Yeah," the landlord said.

He had many examples like that. He'd taken the metal roof off an old shed and used it for the walls of a partly enclosed deck off of the master bedroom: lopsided and crude, strangely silvery and futuristic, with a view of green hills. He'd built a makeshift closet in the smaller bedroom with a homemade rack, plywood shelving, and a shower curtain. He pointed out the skylight in the master bath—"found that in a junk shop for five dollars, installed it the next day"—and the octagonal tiles he'd scavenged from a condemned house downtown.

"You're very resourceful," Isabel said.

She felt a little ridiculous. She was beginning to realize that she was not herself around this man but instead a chirping affirmer. *So strong, so smart, so good at everything!* She didn't know why she was acting like this. This man was her father's age.

A fluffy little Pomeranian—the current tenant's—suddenly bounded down the back stairs and flounced around the landlord's feet, panting with happiness. Then its mood changed and it began growling, nipping at the cuffs of his pants.

"You know how I feel about you," he said to the dog.

Isabel laughed. She crouched down and petted the dog. "Do you have a split personality?" she asked.

The landlord gazed down at them impassively, as though waiting out a storm. Isabel got up. The dog scampered away.

"You're gonna love this," he said. "Let me show you the setup in the basement."

She followed the landlord outside and down a short flight of stairs to the lower entrance. He switched on the light. "Well," he said, the corner of his mouth quirked up, "what do you think of *that*?"

Isabel looked around. The place smelled dank and earthy. It had been converted into an underground bachelor pad, complete with kitchenette, bed, desk, computer, a tiny bathroom cordoned off with rickety Plexiglas borders.

"Wow," she said. She couldn't think of anything else to say.

"And check this out," the landlord said, motioning her over to an elevated area next to the galley kitchen. His voice was full of shy pride. Isabel peeked around the corner and saw an enormous octagonal bathtub on a redwood platform, buffed so the porcelain gleamed. It was easily the cleanest thing in the entire basement.

"That's so cool," Isabel said. She felt exhausted.

"When I'm working on the apartment, I stay down here and just walk on over to my aunt's in the morning," the landlord said. "I figure I might as well be comfortable. My son, he's eighteen, stays down here with me sometimes when he's helping me with projects. Cassie—that's the gal who lives in the house right now—can't even tell we're here, that's what she says. We're just in and out, don't cause her any bother."

Isabel smiled.

"Look at this," he said, turning and snatching something from the window ledge. He showed her an old sallow photograph.

"This was taken when I was about your age, when I first moved to the city," the landlord said. "I was studying violin then, living in an SRO. It was the real artist's life, you know? The real bohemian experience. I imagine that's the stage you're at right now."

Isabel felt, as she took the photograph in her hands, that he had brought her to the basement so he could show her this.

She peered at the picture. A younger version of the land-lord—heavily bearded, slimmer, but with the same blank, dull eyes, and a plaid shirt buttoned to his neck—lolled on a bare mattress, his head propped against the wall. He looked stoned, and much less angry.

"How old are you here?" Isabel asked him.

"Oh, about nineteen. Twenty, maybe."

"I'm twenty-eight," she said. She meant it to come out as casual, incidental, but she got it all wrong. She saw his face darken. "I know I look young," she hastened to add.

He shrugged. "Huh. Yeah, you do look young. I was just guessing."

She flushed. She decided that it would be a mistake to explain further, to tell him she'd only pointed out her age so he'd know she was a responsible adult and not some collegiate party girl. She kept her mouth shut and inhaled the stale damp air.

"My wife grew up in this house," the landlord suddenly announced. "She shared that big downstairs room—the one that's used as a living room now—with her three sisters. And she has four brothers besides." His face briefly lost its harshness and became almost tender.

"Catholic?" Isabel blurted out. Then inwardly she swore at herself: What compelled her to ask this question every time someone mentioned having a big family, as if she herself hadn't been raised Catholic—traditionalist, Vatican II–rejecting Catholic, at that? As if her own parents, an almost-priest and an almost-nun who believed their union had been divinely engineered by Saint Brigid, hadn't practiced birth control. She remembered putting away the laundry one day and finding condoms in her dad's sock drawer. Had she put that in the book? She hadn't.

"I was raised Catholic, that's why I asked," she said.

He shot her a dark sideways look. "Do you go to Mass here?"

"Uh, no," she said. "I don't practice."

Afterward, she couldn't remember how they maneuvered past this awkwardness and emerged into the sunlight, if one of them jump-started the action with a throat-clearing or a grunt, or if they just ascended the stairs like chastened parishioners.

Somehow, they were outside again. She thanked him. And then as she turned to leave the landlord did an odd thing.

"Isabel!" he said, in what seemed unabashed joy and triumph.

He whisked his hand from behind his back and brandished an avocado, one he must have surreptitiously plucked from the backyard tree and squirreled away somewhere on his person. He had conducted the rest of the tour with the green fruit nestled in his pocket like a charm.

"Take it," he said. He was beaming. Isabel smiled back, embarrassed for him.

"Thank you," she said. The fruit was warm and slightly mushy.

She went and sat in a nearby park, a big flat plateau of green overlooking the city. The pastel houses below looked like endless rows of Necco wafers. The park was full of women with baby carriages. When she got up to go, she left the avocado in the grass.

He said he'd call. But after a week passed with no word, Isabel began to worry.

It was May. She had twelve weeks of leisure before she had to teach again, and she was fretful, sleepless, pacing around the ugly apartment with its putty-colored walls, curling linoleum, synthetic-fiber carpet that stuck straight up like a cheap doll's hair.

Isabel was supposed to be working on her next book. But she didn't want to write it. She didn't know what more she had to say. She told herself that if she could just get settled someplace decent, she'd be able to concentrate. She left a mes-

sage on the landlord's voice mail, sitting at her desk in a bath-
robe, trying to sound crisp and busy: "Hi, Glenn, this is Isabel,
the girl you showed the house to last week. I really loved the
place and, um, I was just calling to check in and see how the
process is coming along." She thanked him and recited her
number into the receiver.

After days passed and he didn't call, she began to imagine
paranoid scenarios.

"I know what happened," she told her friend Andy over
coffee. "He looked me up, went and read my book, and was
horrified."

"By your life?" Andy said.

"No," said Isabel, "by my eagerness to graphically disclose
it."

Andy paused and stirred his coffee. "It's not graphic."

"Yeah, well, it doesn't matter, because I know this type of
guy. This kind of old-school, stoic guy who believes you don't
air your dirty laundry in public, that it's a weakness and it
means you're unstable. Plus I think he's Catholic. So he's got
to hate me."

Andy said, "You think the Pope sent out an alert to all par-
ishes? With your face on it? Like in the post office?"

Isabel said, "Well, I committed blasphemy, after all. Or sac-
rilege. Or both."

"Please," Andy said. "Who's the Pope to judge? He was in
the *Jungvolk*, for Christ's sake."

Andy was a lapsed Catholic, too, although his defection had
more to do with indifference than self-imposed banishment.
He was a round blond man, endearingly bearish, who unself-
consciously danced with his wife in public and treated Isabel

like a pesky but beloved little sister, although they were the same age. They had met when he profiled Isabel for the local arts magazine, where he worked as a features editor. The profile began with this sentence: *At age nine, while most children in her Michigan hometown were ice-fishing and raising hogs for 4-H, Isabel Hyde was becoming a modern-day Julian of Norwich.*

No one in her town ice-fished or raised hogs.

"Well," Isabel said, "it's driving me crazy. This place is my dream house. If my nine-year-old self saw this house, she'd lose her shit."

"Didn't you say the landlord lives in the basement?" Andy said. "Isn't that kind of creepy?"

"He doesn't live there," Isabel snapped. "He just stays there when he's doing repairs on the other place. Besides, I'd rather have some guy in the basement than drunks pissing all over the street and passing out."

"Really?" Andy said. He seemed genuinely surprised. "You'd rather have a guy in the basement?"

Isabel walked home, annoyed. Andy and Beth lived in a beautiful rent-controlled flat near the ocean with huge windows and built-in bookcases and a garden. Plus, they had each other. She decided not to call Andy for a few days.

An old man ambled toward her on the sidewalk. He was dressed like a weekend golfer in khaki shorts and athletic socks and a bright polo shirt, his hair white and groomed. He stopped to address her. She thought he needed directions.

"You're a human piece of shit," the old man said. He looked her straight in the eye, his face a scrubbed pink dumpling, his blue eyes watery and clear. "Nothing but a human piece of shit."

Isabel walked away from him. Her hands shook as she unlocked her front door, even as she told herself it was dumb to feel personally offended by someone who was out of his mind.

She made chamomile tea and tried to relax. She checked her voice mail: nothing. She checked her email, and that's where she found it, buried in her inbox with the junk mail and announcements of readings and multiple notes from her editor with the subject line *checking in*: a message from the landlord.

Isabel stared at the boldfaced subject line—**House**—and put her cup down. Her stomach felt like a whirlpool. She couldn't remember giving the landlord her email, but she must have put it on the application. She clicked on it.

Hi Isabel. Glenn here. Thanks for your interest in the house as well as the apartment that you saw earlier. Coming from a creative artist such as yourself, I consider it a compliment. My initial impressions of you were that you were practical yet funky. And as such would like the house with all of its special touches. But after reading your application, doing an online search, and taking a look at your published book, I became aware that you are as well an intense artist and a complicated person who perhaps would require a more vital environment than this neighborhood would provide. Upon discussion, my wife agreed with me. My wife is friendly with a young engaged couple looking for a prenuptial nest, and we decided that they would be a better fit.

As an artist, violinist, who dropped out of college and moved to San Francisco because I needed stimulation for my art, may I suggest you try the Tenderloin? Don't laugh. With some self-defense spray and your intense awareness you'd be OK.

May your creative energies stay focused. Don't forget all great artists have one thing in common. Imagination, and you've got that in spades.

Isabel read the message twice. Twenty minutes passed before she was able to compose a terse note in response, thanking the landlord for his time and consideration. Then she called Andy.

"I was right," she said. "He 'researched' me and got scared off."

Andy said, "He's the one that sounds a little scary. 'Prenuptial nest'? And all that shit about researching you? I think you dodged a bullet."

"I don't even know," Isabel said. To her dismay, her throat felt hot and thick. "I'm starting to think it's me. That I'm just doomed to exile."

Andy told her she was being ridiculous and that she'd find a better place.

After hanging up, Isabel crawled into bed and lay on her back, looking up at the ceiling. Her stomach burned the way it had when she was ten years old, right before she finally came clean.

She'd begun coughing up blood in the cafeteria, a development that initially only heightened her mystique. But it had terrified her. It was the beginning of the end. Her parents drove her to the ER, where she was promptly diagnosed with a bleeding ulcer. On the way home, she broke down and confessed that she'd made it all up: the visions, the Virgin Mary in her pale-blue snood, the trances and the dreams. And then everything changed. One life ended, and she began the next.

Isabel got out of bed and opened the cabinet where she kept the old review copies of the memoir. She didn't like looking at the book. She couldn't help seeing it through the adopted gaze of the landlord, and she cringed at the cover, that infamous picture of herself from an old issue of the *Heartland Catholic Reader*: nine years old, in a white First Communion dress, barefoot in the grass behind the school- yard, pointing toward the vacant lot where she claimed the Virgin had appeared. The photo was captioned, *Fatima of the Midwest*.

She flipped through and found the ulcer section. She'd devoted five pages to it. "What I didn't tell them," she had written, "was that, at that moment, I believed more intensely than I ever had before. I believed that my body bled to purge itself of darkness and heaviness, to hollow out a place for light, so that I could ascend. I'd been pretending so long that I lost sight of what was real and what was made up, and I came to truly believe that bodies were capable of ideological fidelity. That a corpse could smell of lilies. That eyes can weep blood, and palms and feet sprout mysterious wounds. That the flesh was a reflection of the soul. And this terrified me, because there was no limit to how far it could go. I was ready for it to stop—all of it, all."

Isabel closed the book. The thing she had just read seemed like a noisily patterned towel hung to conceal someone undressing behind it, half naked and ignominious. What she hadn't written, what it had never occurred to her to describe, was what she remembered now: the stunning isolation of non- belief. She remembered the convulsive fear that seized her when the blood bubbled up, a fear not only of dying but of the possibility that they would *let* her die, that they would just keep staring, transfixed and exultant, as her lungs drowned. In a scalding flash of panic, it occurred to her that every adult in town had gone crazy: her parents and neighbors, her teachers, even the police. They believed she had seen visions and their belief rendered her, in their eyes, supernatural and impervious to harm.

It had all started when Isabel told one of her teachers at St. Stephen's that she had seen the Virgin Mary. It was a wild, attention-seeking whim, perhaps motivated by a fleeting intimation of punishment in the teacher's demeanor, perhaps by Isabel having been picked last in kickball that day. She said the Virgin had a thin face and was not especially beautiful, but her voice was high and sweet and there was rosy light radiating from her in points, like she was faceted, diamondlike. She also seemed very hurt, Isabel told the teacher, as though she were watching the death of something gentle and defenseless and was powerless to stop it.

Things might have gone no further had Isabel not added that, according to the Virgin, someone closely connected to St. Stephen's would be in heaven soon. Three days later the parish priest, an ancient man who had worked alongside Mother Teresa in his heyday, keeled over from a heart attack while saying Mass.

Things snowballed, aided by timing and coincidence. A tornado wheeled through town that summer, destroying the south side of town and leveling a Catholic hospital that sold religious ceramic figurines in its gift shop; among the rubble were found several miniature reproductions of Michelangelo's *Pietà*, totally intact except, in some cases, for Jesus' feet. And then Isabel's fourth-grade class made a pilgrimage to Grosse Pointe for the once-in-a-lifetime chance to see the Pope say Mass at St. Paul on the Lake Parish. At one point the Pope called all the children who had been affected by the tornado to stand in front of the altar for a blessing, and he cupped Isabel's face in his papery hands—an intimate moment captured disingenuously on the JumboTron installed for the occasion—and then seemed to linger over her, perhaps to whisper in her ear. In reality, he had merely bent forward and wheezed for a moment. But the die was cast, and the town believed it had been chosen, and even Isabel's parents began to look at her uneasily.

She was an ideal vessel: delicate, saturnine of aspect, with a mournful face and an eerie, shell-shocked poise. She had always been like that. Her endurance was the stuff of legend: no one could crouch in an uncomfortable hiding spot longer than she, or stay as unnervingly motionless in a game of freeze-tag. The inanimate quality of her stillness made her unusually approachable by animals. She was an eccentric, lonely child, given to soulful gazing and cryptic pronouncements. Her accounts of divine apparitions, relayed with hushed restraint, were random and idiosyncratic enough to be credible.

And she knew this, even as a child. She knew it instinctively, without calculation, just as she knew, as an adult, that she would make a much more sympathetic figure if she had truly believed. If she had been an innocent, brainwashed by religious mania, whose desperate bid for love and acceptance had led her unwittingly into wide-scale fraud, the whole episode would be forgivable—moreover, it would make some

sort of sense. And that was what the Isabel of the memoir provided: an explanation, a *why*, a little girl who fooled herself as
much as anyone else.

She stuck the book back in the file cabinet and shut the
drawer.

A couple days later, the landlord left a phone message while
she was out. His voice was leaden and rough. He said, "Isabel,
Glenn here. I don't know if you've come to your senses yet or
if you're still interested in the house, but I managed to convince my wife you'd be a far better tenant than the engaged
couple. She saw my reasoning. So it's yours if you want it, for
certain this time."

There was something smug and deadened in his voice—*I
managed to convince my wife*—and Isabel knew she didn't want
to see the man again. Still, she was tempted by visions of that
house.

"Do yourself a favor," Andy said when she told him, "and
do not respond to this guy. He's too much of a whack job, and
he lives in the basement. Please."

And Isabel, though tempted by the offer, had bitched so
much to Andy about the landlord's inappropriate email that
she would lose face if she took the place now, and she didn't
want Andy to think she'd been complaining just for the sake
of complaining. "Yeah, I know," she said. "I won't. It's just
. . . the house. You know? But I'm over it."

Two weeks passed. Isabel read a lot, played solitaire on
the computer, ended up sleeping most of the day. She got
into the habit of drinking in the wee hours—not much, just
a nightly scotch and soda. It was after one of these nights—

midday with the sunlight streaming through the picture window and her head tender and pulsing with hangover—that she received another email from the landlord. Its subject line was *Communication as Consummation.*

Isabel clicked on it and saw that it was several paragraphs long. It began:

> *My Beautiful, Darling Isabel,*
>
> *Your instincts are correct, but your intuition is inchoate. My intentions were honorable, however. If you will excuse one last breech into familiarity so as to set the record straight and attempt to remedy any further injury that only imagined injustices can inflict.*
>
> *There is always the potential when a man and woman meet for a life altering event to take place. Where one party is left overwhelmed and unable to continue on as before. Such occurred on April 19, when a naïve young woman, seemingly unaware of her own enchantment and power, innocently befriended a man whose life had long since steered into one of banal existence.*

Isabel sat back, then leaned forward again. She felt a queasy sense of suspension, as if waiting for the inevitable punch line to a joke at her expense. But it didn't come.

> *As he was telling her about the closet in the rental property, he noticed her flinch with her eyes. This is a very fragile girl, he thought and immediately a feeling of sympathy and protectiveness came over him. He will always be protective of her, not like a father, but more like a grandfather, with adoration and worship. She was the closest thing to Jane Eyre that he will ever encounter. He would have done anything within his means to protect her. In his ultimate fantasy he*

saw her as the lyricist for his imagined musical based on the Damnation of Faust.

Since you only know how much you love something when you tell it goodbye, it is a rare luxury to be prescient at the final moment of any relationship. Had I known on that Sunday when you left the house. That final touch, that final glimpse, that final sound of your voice. They would have been embedded in my consciousness forever. But now they are lost, and this is all that remains. Goodbye.

She laughed.

How could she not? The melodrama. *The Damnation of Faust.* How he referred to himself in the third person. It was so over-the-top that for several seconds she just sat in front of the computer, openmouthed, on the verge of giddiness, murmuring, *What the fuck?* As if someone were there with her. And her first impulse was to find a witness. It was how she'd felt after her book had been accepted for publication—the feeling of having received a bizarrely random tribute, one that was predicated on someone's false perception of her.

Andy was at work. Isabel's other friends in the city were colleagues at the college; they didn't know her very well. But she wanted to be among other people, away from the computer.

She stepped outside. The sun was bright and the street smelled of stale piss. The usual group of day laborers played cards on the corner. She walked several blocks to a coffee shop, slipping in and out of crowds of uniformed children, squalling drunks, ragged men and women pushing shopping carts, baby-faced hipsters in 1940s vintage. She felt an irrational need to collar someone, anyone, even the drunks and the children, and blurt out what had happened. Preface it with, *Tell me what I'm supposed to think of this.* But instead she ordered black tea and sat on a bench outside the café. She watched the people.

After a few minutes, her eyes filled with tears. She tried to stanch them, but they overflowed and ran down her face. She reacted as she would have to a bout of public incontinence: pulled her coat tightly around her and walked home as quickly as possible.

Isabel lived in quasi-denial about her memoir being a memoir. She hated to see it shelved alongside dreary accounts of addiction and disease and familial disgrace. Her favorite author, a dead man, a writer's writer, called these books the "Look, Ma, I'm Breathing" genre: disclosure for the sake of disclosure.

But she never would have written her story as fiction. It *was* disclosure for the sake of disclosure. She *wanted* people to know what she'd done. She wanted people to look her in the eye and talk to her while knowing full well she'd masqueraded as a seer, debunked her own myth as handily as she'd perpetuated it, and restored the town to jaded sanity. And then resurrected herself from disgrace and recorded it all with such brittle and parched restraint that no one, not even the most cynical, could accuse her of exaggerating. She wanted people to squirm under the weight of it, knowing they couldn't bring up her past in any but a literary context, knowing that, eternally, she had the last word. A last word with a large print run.

The book ended with a description of the last time she went to Mass, when, on a whim, she walked into a Catholic church in the city she was living in. She was nineteen and estranged from her parents. There were only a few people in the pews.

The priest faced the congregation. As he presided over the sacrament of transubstantiation, his rote competence struck her as banal as a vacuum salesman's pitch. He seemed like a nice man. She sat through the whole Mass unmoved, and walked out of the building into the sunlight with a condensed impression, finally, of why they had been willing to believe her.

She wrote:

Their credulity was not a testament to the power of my performance. Rather, it was a testament to their own need: for a sign, a perfect symbol, an infusion of hot, surging blood into their tepid and watered-down rituals. What I had done was undeniably harmful. But the harm they did, by believing me, was irreparable—to me, to themselves, to their children. As I sat in the unfamiliar church and watched an eleven-year-old girl take Communion, extending her tongue for the host, I knew it could happen again. They were still hungry for it. This girl met my gaze as she walked down the aisle to her pew. She was wan-faced, her eyes large and preternaturally grave. And instead of warning her, *You could be next*, I got up and walked out into the sunlight. The freshness of the outside air was an exhilarating contrast to the frankincense musk of the church. I walked faster and faster and didn't stop. I must have been halfway home by the time the girl, my last and most chilling apparition, knelt for the final hymn, eyes shut tight, waiting for the words that signaled her freedom: *Go in peace to love and serve the Lord.*

That wasn't true. There had been no little girl.
What she'd really thought was, looking around the tired and

sparse congregation, *I forgive them*. And then realized there was
no need to. Her parents, the Church, her teachers, the neighbors: she had already forgiven all of them. It was easy to forgive
the people she had hoodwinked and left behind. The people
she couldn't forgive were those who had left *her* behind. Almost
everyone she had slept with. The friends who'd moved away,
gotten married, and left her alone. The inhabitants of her new,
secularized world, who had received her devotion and her con-
fessions with utter and affable indifference. None had victim-
ized her. None had been committed enough to victimize her.

Perhaps this was why, as the landlord continued to email, she
did not feel angry. Not even threatened. Not at first. Just abuzz
with a disturbing, nauseating curiosity, as though turning over a
boulder to see the mess of grubs and worms. No, she wasn't
exactly angry. He had not been stoic, after all; he had been
moved. He had brazenly shone a light on her vulnerability: *This
is a very fragile girl.* Then, instead of recoiling, he drew closer.

She didn't want him to come closer. But she did not feel
entitled to push him away.

The next email came three days after the last.

> *Isabel,*
>
> *No I won't just go softly into the night. Not when there is a
> greater need afloat. I was at the DMV today, and saw all the ugli-
> ness and ignorance and thought of you and how the fine should look
> out for each other. I want to be your bodyguard, but first you must
> trust me, so I want to establish my pedigree with you.*

Isabel rubbed her eyes. It was four in the morning; her sleep
patterns had been disrupted by too much daytime napping.

The email had been sent a mere twenty minutes earlier. She shivered. She imagined the landlord in the basement of the rental house, fortified by the nobility of his mission, typing away as the tenant and tiny dog slept upstairs. She wondered if he had some way of telling how quickly his emails were read.

The landlord followed his opening declaration with a multi-paragraph litany of vital statistics: birth date, parents' occupations, high school years, SAT scores, significant relationships. His career trajectory. How he and Isabel were ninety degrees apart on the Zodiac: *Probably one reason I understood you so quickly.* Next was a list of admirable personal qualities: perseverance, loyalty, enormous powers of concentration.

> *And my new project, Isabel, is you: your well-being, your happiness. You are just too fine a commodity to allow to be ravaged by the baser forces at play in this town. Of all the things I liked about you, I think it's your joy that I remember the most. You walking down the sidewalk that morning, your green shirt on, and the smile on your face when you saw me. You looked like a little girl delighted to meet her fate. You looked 15.*

A week later came the email that ended it. She was almost relieved as she read it. He'd snapped at last. It was like a fever breaking. There was no salutation.

> *Your silence has given me the opportunity to reflect. I'm starting to hate you. I had an insight today, listening to your phone message of a month ago. You're a chameleon. You sounded hot in that message. You definitely were working me. Oozing charm in every inflection and intonation. You wanted this house. You sounded like a*

whore, the ultimate opportunist. Not the precious fragile girl I had
met the day before. Given your history, I should have known from
the beginning. You were playing me.

He went on in this vein for several paragraphs, impugning
her lack of integrity, her sluttish manipulations, her black and
empty soul and the barrenness of her heart, the animus underlying her cultivated mien, her martyr complex. And then,
finally, there was this:

When their innate vulnerability is denied, that is when women
start to idealize being hurt. Being punished. You wanted to be a
martyr. To suffer. Because of Catholicism? Some conditioned craving
for expiation? I don't think so. No matter what you tried to make
yourself believe as you wrote that book. You picked the easy answer.
But I can see the truth. What you wanted was to be protected. What
you needed was for your fragility to be affirmed. It wasn't. Simple as
that. And so you lied. And you became what you are today: a white
slave in a Chinese whorehouse. Convincing each master he's the
best. Whatever it takes to survive.

Isabel shut off her computer. She went to the bathroom and
threw up. When there was nothing left she kept dry-heaving
until something stirred in her, like a small foot put down gently.

She got up from the floor and brushed her teeth. She turned
the computer back on and printed out each email from the
landlord, one by one, and looked up the county clerk's Web
site. She dressed in her severest and most asexual clothing:
black pants, gray button-down that accentuated the flatness of
her chest, clunky boots. Then she walked outside, stepped

over blocks of passed-out bodies, and took the bus downtown
to the courthouse.

The building's exterior was white and tiered as a wedding
cake, but the inside looked sterile and joyless. Isabel had to fill
out five separate forms. It felt as if she were writing the same
information over and over again.

The clerk, a young Hispanic woman with long nails and
wavy, copper-highlighted hair, told her what to do. There
were other women in the room, too, filling out Requests for
Orders to Stop Harassment; Isabel was the most dressed-up
and looked younger than all of them. At first this made her
nervous, but as she stepped forward and committed herself to
the process, an old self-preserving reflex took over: a restrained
bravado that made her look the clerk in the eye, refuse to
apologize for not being worse off or battered or poor. She
filled out the exhaustive forms with lucid encapsulations and in
impeccable penmanship. She filled out the civil harassment
report. Then filled out the request. Then applied for the fee
waiver and the petition to have the sheriff serve the papers. *I
would like the court to serve him,* she wrote. *I do not want to ask any
family member or friend to have contact with this man; he's clearly
volatile and unpredictable.*

Months later she would reread the papers, struck by the
desperate pomposity of her language, and cringe.

The clerk took the papers and said, "So the next step is to
come back in three hours after they've been filed and endorsed
by the Superior Court. And then you'll receive your date for
the hearing."

"Is he going to be at the hearing?" Isabel said.

The clerk said, "He has the option to be."

"Will he be able to talk to me?"

"No," the clerk said, shaking her head. "He isn't allowed to address you directly. You'll sit in separate sections of the courtroom. There's a bailiff present. Everything's very controlled."

The clerk's dark eyes were wide and kind.

"I want to minimize contact with him as much as possible."

"He probably won't even show up," the clerk said. "A lot of times they don't."

When everything was filed and endorsed, Isabel didn't want to go home. She thought of her computer, its ON button glowing neon-green in the corner of the living room. She couldn't think of where to go.

When she finally showed up at Andy and Beth's front door, she immediately launched into a defense of her presence before Beth could even say hello.

"I'm sorry for dropping in on you," Isabel said. "It's just that I don't feel comfortable going home right now. This man's been stalking me, and I just filed a restraining order, and he knows where I live, and I just need to be somewhere other than there. If you can just let me sit in your living room and read or something for a while. I won't get in your way."

Beth's eyes widened. She opened the door. "Isabel, *what*? What? Get in here."

Their house was quiet and warm and orderly. There was a cat and a fireplace. Tacked to the fridge was a handwritten schedule of whose turn it was to cook, and which recipe from the *Moosewood Cookbook* would be used. The walls, a warm brick-red, felt safely enclosing. Beth brought her a cup of tea.

"Andy's still at work," she said. She looked tired, with grooves under her eyes and her straw-colored hair loose.

Isabel had always felt intimidated by Beth, who was tall and willowy and had been raised by missionaries in Uganda and spoke three languages. Isabel explained what was happening in her most moderate tone, not wanting to sound like an overreacting writer, worried that Beth wouldn't believe her, that Beth suspected her of trying to seduce Andy, even though Beth made sympathetic noises and touched Isabel's knee during the creepiest parts, as if they were watching a horror movie together.

"Something kind of like that happened to me once," Beth said when Isabel finished.

"Really? What?"

"Well," Beth said, adjusting her skirt and scooting closer to Isabel on the floor, "this was when Andy and I were dating. It was this wacko who lived in the Catholic Charities shelter across the courtyard from my building. The guy would jerk off sitting in his windowsill. Then he tried to break in one night when I was sleeping. And after that I never really lived there again. I had to break my lease, move in with Andy, and this guy loitered around the front of the building the whole time I was moving. I thought, seriously, Andy was going to kill him."

Isabel looked at her. "Jesus Christ," she said. "Well, now I feel comparatively lucky."

Beth shook her head. "I don't know. The person you're dealing with has access to your personal information. And he's much more articulate and self-possessed."

Isabel felt a sudden urge to be close to Beth. She wanted to scoot into the curve of her lean strong arm, put her head on her shoulder, ask her if she was sure, positive, that Isabel was a good person, a person who didn't deserve this, a person not at fault.

She wondered if Beth had ever read her book.

"This makes me want to go back and change the book," she blurted out. "Change everything in it."

"Your book?" Beth said. "Why?"

"Because," Isabel said, "I keep picturing him reading it. It makes me seem so cold and hard. And I was never like that. I don't want people thinking they can hurt me and I won't feel it. They read that, they think I'm immune to everything. And I'm such a fucking mess. I want to write a book called *I'm a Fucking Mess, Now Leave Me Alone.* You know?"

Beth laughed. And so it all came off as gallows humor, Isabel making a self-deprecating joke to defuse the intensity, and she could tell Beth was relieved; Beth had been worried she would break down.

"I need to work on my lesson plan for tomorrow, honey," Beth said, "but you can totally stay here, okay? As long as you need." She squeezed Isabel's shoulder.

When Andy came home, they all had dinner. They discussed the upcoming hearing.

Andy said, "You're going to verbally eviscerate him in front of that judge. He'll be sorry he was ever born."

Beth added, "He's fucking with the wrong girl."

"He has no idea what he's in for," Andy said. He chuckled. "It's going to be awesome."

Isabel looked down at her salad. Then she looked up and smiled.

"Yes," she said.

The night before the hearing, she wrote down everything she wanted to say. She ironed her outfit: a button-down pink shirt and gray pants, the ensemble of a postcollegiate interviewee.

Her strategy was to look as young as possible while sounding as old as possible.

Andy and Beth drove her to the courthouse. They both took the morning off work. Isabel was touched at how they stuck by her, flanking her on either side like parents, their faces wary and more serious than she had ever seen them. They kept scanning the crowds.

Isabel spotted the landlord as she waited in line to give the clerk her case number and sign in. There were at least twenty other civil harassment cases being heard in the same courtroom, and offenders and accusers lingered uneasily in the same line, not speaking. It was easy to tell which was which. The accusers were mostly female and had someone, if only a courtappointed advocate, with them. The offenders were all male and unaccompanied, with haunted, defensive eyes. They did not look prepared.

Neither did the landlord. She was surprised to find him much slighter than she remembered, without his tool belt and jeans. And his air of gruff authority was completely deflated. He looked shell-shocked. His face was unshaven and sallow, his hair mussed, and he wore all white: a stained white T-shirt and white sweatpants. He stood six people ahead of Isabel in line. She pointed him out to Andy and Beth.

Andy craned his neck. "What does he think he is, a Hare Krishna?" he said.

"My God," Beth whispered, "what a creep. He looks deranged."

Isabel kept her head down as they filed into the courtroom. It was completely full. The defendants sat on one side and the plaintiffs on the other. In front of the judge's bench was a long table with two chairs and a microphone on each end. The bailiff told everyone to stand, and the judge entered the room. She swam in her black gown, a small middle-aged woman with short curly hair like Isabel's mother's.

"Good," Beth whispered. "It's a woman."

There were eight cases before Isabel's. The first to testify was a young black woman who kept one elbow on the table with her keys loosely in her fist and gestured, jangling, while she talked. The defendant wasn't there.

"Obviously he can't understand that 'restraining order' means 'stay away.' This got renewed once already, and he still keeps coming around, to where I work, to the house, while I'm alone with the kids, and I'm thinking he is never going to leave me alone." Underneath the fear and strain in the woman's voice was a pragmatic, frustrated intelligence breaking through like cracks of light.

Isabel looked down at her notes, feeling sick. What was she doing here, wasting taxpayer money, a bourgeois lightweight spooked by objectionable emails? She licked her lips and read:

> I was disturbed, not only because this man is my father's age with grown children and is a virtual stranger to me, but because he is so estranged from reality as to construct a narrative of intimacy and attachment based on absolutely nothing.

It seemed so impossibly formal. She stole a glance at the landlord's yellowish, vacant-eyed face across the aisle. He was watching the woman speak, watching her walk away from the table and talk to the bailiff after getting her order renewed for another three years. He sat through the next six cases with the same lack of expression. And when Isabel's name was called, his was called with it, and Andy patted her shoulder and hissed, "Kill him," and she knew, with weary inevitability, that she would.

Isabel and the landlord sat down at opposite ends of the table. It was like a game show without buzzers. They didn't look at each other as the judge leaned forward and said, "Ms. Hyde, would you make a statement explaining why you filed this request?"

Isabel bent her head toward the microphone and began to speak. She felt the landlord staring at her. She kept looking up at the judge, watching the woman's face change as she unspooled her long memorized sentences, hands folded in front of her, voice high and flat and sweet. She relished the jolt on the judge's face. She thought of how she must look next to this haggard, jowly, unkempt man: tiny and neat as a bandbox figure, chillingly youthful. *You looked 15.*

She talked and talked. She was conscious of using the phrase "estranged from reality" several times; she switched to "lacking in rational judgment." She ended with, "I filed this order not because I felt my life was in danger, but because I wanted to prevent his behavior from escalating further, to nip this in the bud before it grew completely out of control."

Then it was the landlord's turn to respond. He sighed. He shuffled the papers in front of him, slumped in his seat, and cleared his throat with a phlegmy croak.

"I had hoped," he said, looking down, "that the emails would provide a dialogue between us. I never expressed a sexual desire for her. I offered to help her and hoped for a friendship. Only my final email would have alarmed a normal person, and even in that one I was trying to serve a legitimate purpose. She told me she was a Catholic. I assumed she understood guilt." He coughed. "Her book—she wrote a book, it's widely available, out there for public consumption"—the contempt in his voice brought a reflexive, close-lipped smirk to her face—"and it makes a point about masochism, especially among females. I provided a theoretical and sociological explanation for why certain girls and young women have this problem, to start a dialogue."

He raised his voice. "Your Honor, it's excerpts like these that invite communication about these issues. *The nuns and brothers were not sadists.*" He kept going, his voice becoming more forceful, measured, staccato, like a filibustering senator quoting the Constitution. With a horrible start, Isabel realized he was reading from her memoir.

"They did not enjoy paddling children, and it was their obvious reluctance and distaste that snapped me out of my repeat-offender stupor quicker than a real beating ever could. I would have preferred the worst physical pain to this grudging, put-upon delivery, this intimation that they and not I were suffering the real punishment."

He had a copy of her book in his hands. The judge looked at Isabel, almost involuntarily. The little girl on the cover pointed across the vacant lot, in Isabel's direction.

"Now," the landlord continued, slapping it shut, "this is a girl who fabricated divine visitations of the Virgin Mary. And, not coincidentally, she fantasized from the age of five about being beaten. This is all in the book. It seemed notable to me that there's a connection between this denial of her own vulnerability and the masochism of this martyr act she embarked

upon. She didn't tie them together in the book. All I was trying to do was bring it to her attention, as a reporter might do
while interviewing."

"Sir," the judge began. "Sir, you've said—"

"I wasn't threatening," the landlord said. His voice wavered.
"I never threatened her, that's the last thing I'm going to say,
I'm sorry, Your Honor."

There was a pause. Then the judge said, "Ms. Hyde, do you
want to respond?"

Isabel looked up at her helplessly: her black robe like a cler-
ic's, her rimless glasses, and the eyes behind them. For a
moment she was so overcome with shame she wanted to run
out of the room. Then she thought of Andy, behind her. How
he probably wished he could storm the bench and do this for
her. Isabel found her anger where it always was. She sat up
straight and stiff.

"I think," she said, "his defense of his actions as stemming
from some attempt to initiate 'dialogue' with me is baseless. I
never mentioned my writing to him, never invited his feedback or response. My being the author of a book doesn't justify these intrusive and unwanted personal attentions and it
doesn't mean I invited them. What he wrote was of a personal
nature. It was not a book review. He called me a Chinese
whore."

That just popped out. Then she remembered, aghast, that
he had called her a *white* whore in a Chinese whorehouse. She
half expected him to correct her. She pointed her eyes down
to signify she was done.

The judge cleared her throat and said, "All right. The
restraining order is granted for three years. Under this order

the accused cannot come within fifty feet of the complainant, cannot call, email, write, or otherwise initiate contact with her, without facing imprisonment. Mr. Elkin, you are free to go; Ms. Hyde, please wait a moment for your paperwork."

The landlord got up and shuffled out. She saw the bailiff, a large black man, stop him at the door and confer with him in a curt, revolted way, using choppy hand gestures, eyes wide and wary as a hostage negotiator's. She couldn't look anymore. He had left her book on the table.

Andy and Beth took her out to lunch to celebrate.

"You were great," Beth said. "You handled yourself so well."

"He threw me," Isabel said. "With the book thing."

"Well, he shot himself in the foot," Andy said, "because that just proved he was nuts. It's like some psycho waving around a Britney Spears album and claiming her lyrics were speaking to him."

"Except Britney Spears doesn't sing about being a precocious fake martyr. Unless there's a subtext I'm not getting."

They didn't laugh. Isabel didn't expect them to. She kept eating her salad.

"It doesn't matter what the book said," Andy told her. "He had no right."

They ate for a while in silence. Isabel looked at Andy. She knew he'd read the book, and she assumed Beth had, but neither had ever discussed it with her. It was embarrassment, she knew, and respect. They liked her; they didn't want to think of her doing bad things, hurting other people or herself. Now she saw they were also ashamed for her. And she knew the

landlord had given the most emotionally charged and forth-
coming response the book would ever receive—peerless in its
fierce claim on her attention, its reckless disregard of her
reserve, and unforgivable.

Isabel looked down at her plate.

"Well," she said, "my next book is going to be a treatise on
the mating habits of the dung beetle. Fuck this shit."

They laughed harder than they needed to.

Isabel found a new apartment on the opposite side of town, an
affordable place with a coin-op laundry in the basement and an
elderly landlady who called her Imogene. Andy and Beth
helped her move. Fall semester began and she put on her professional clothes and tied her hair back and taught her classes,
the students peering at her with curiosity and deference, having read the book, subdued by the knowledge of her horrible
actions. She felt relatively normal.

Her editor kept calling about the new book. First she asked
for a hundred pages. Then she asked for fifty.

"Anything you can give me," she said. "We can't extend
the deadline much longer, Isabel."

Isabel didn't know how to answer. A dreamy inertia settled
over her whenever she thought about the new book.

"I've got ideas," she said slowly. "I've got ideas."

And she did, vaguely. She thought of doing a biography of
her namesake, St. Isabel of Portugal, who had lived a tranquil
and nonbloody life, as far as saints' lives went. But deep down
she knew she couldn't write the life story of anyone other than
herself. Then she tried to get all fired up about some global
injustice, so she could write a passionate screed about it. But

the news—war, genocide, rape, species nearing extinction—just made her feel helpless and stupid.

She taught her classes and took a lot of walks. She got in the habit of tackling the new book very late at night, after grading papers, with a glass of scotch in one hand, leaning against the headboard with the computer in her lap and waiting to have something to say. But her mind always wandered back to the hearing. The landlord all in white. Her silky pink shirt with its itchy tag. Most of all she thought of herself at the very moment she started to speak, before he had brought out the book and shamed her. How she opened her mouth and things came out, elegant and lucid things, and she was like the nightingale in the fairy tale placed in front of the king, watching respect and recognition dawn on the judge's face—this doll-like girl, she speaks so well!—watching the stenographer look up at her for an instant and grimace sympathetically, that subtle empathy women convey like a shoulder-squeeze, and, surrounded by the blank walls of her new apartment, she held the scotch in one hand and knew it was useless, knew that nothing would ever come out of her more purely or clearly than things like this: these distilled episodes, these illuminated lamentations, sculpted in all the right places, these testimonies of harm.

consummation

Twenty-seven years ago, when you were a surgical intern at Bingham Medical Center in Paw Paw, Michigan, you saved my father's life. He was not your patient. And although he, too, worked at Bingham—as director of the nephrology laboratory—the two of you never crossed paths there. The moment at which you saved his life did not take place in a hospital at all, but in the master bedroom of our vinyl-sided ranch on Paley Road, directly across the street from the red-brick split-level you shared with your wife during the tenure of your residency. It was a month before the tornado.

It must have been disconcerting when my mother knocked on your door that morning. You knew her, I suppose, in the way you must have known my father, with a certain uncon-scious gratitude for the consistency of her persona: the woman across the street who waved from her lawn, fixed as a model in a seasonal catalogue spread, posing through cycles of snow-clearing and mowing and gardening. She was a schoolteacher. She spoke with the brisk hand-clapping pragmatism of someone who spent a lot of time around very young children, but she could not tell us what was wrong with our father, and she couldn't tell you, either. What was wrong with him defied classification. There was a renegade volatility to it, like a bewitchment or a biblical plague. She ushered you through the foyer and past the bookshelves and server, past Jane and me and through the white-painted double doors leading to the hallway, and she must have said, in the well-bred embarrassed way of someone unaccustomed to making requests, "Can you just look at him?"

If it were a hospital you would have opened the door and breezed in and started confidently prognosticating. But it was a home and there were children; all around you were the smells of lives having been led for years without serious interruption until this fissure, this pox visited improbably upon a modest peach-colored ranch house bought for $15,000 in 1970, a house that looked too inconsequential for a pox to have taken the trouble, a house indistinguishable from hundreds of others in a frumpily virtuous neighborhood skirting the edge between middle-class and lower-middle-class, a neighborhood you escaped from as soon as you started making real money, Doctor, and then it was off to Portage and the executive homes.

I imagine you were polite, and that you knocked on the bedroom door, announced your name, and that he invited you in. Perhaps this unnerved you—his voice weak and croaky from disuse, rising valiantly in a blind adherence to social proprieties and the strongest survival instinct in my father's arsenal: the ability to put others at ease. I'm sure the voice sounded ashamed—desperately reassuring, but ashamed—as if the man inside were urgently adjusting his position in preparation for your arrival, although he knew full well it didn't matter and that nothing could wipe the shock off your face once you entered the room and saw his body on top of the bedclothes, naked except for underwear.

The initial associations one typically makes, when meeting someone in his condition, are apocalyptic: scenes of atrocity and torture and nuclear warfare, Hiroshima, Chernobyl. His lips were almost indistinguishable from the crusted, ravaged jelly of the rest of his face, his eyeballs dark yellow, his skinny body glowing red as sunburn. But the redness seemed unconfined to the epidermis, originating in some molten seething core that irradiated organs and muscles and bones and skin from the inside out. And unlike the scorched texture of sunburn this redness gleamed raw as a flayed carcass, moist and weeping, mangled by blisters.

He would have said hello to you and called you by name and made haste to cover himself, my father, courteous above measure, with a refinement that thrived on understatement. Maybe no one had died on you yet and you thought he might be the first. I imagine it was disorienting to be suddenly plucked off your front porch and whisked into the bedroom of a couple you barely knew, the room thick with the humid smell of their sleep, their open closet filled with white lab coats and holey bathrobes, housecoats and sheepskin scuffs with matted heels, the wall over their bed hung with a painting of the Virgin Mary in which she looked like Maria Callas, swarthy and operatic. Their child at the door suddenly, a thumb in her mouth: my sister Jane. My father said, "Get her out." I know that tone, low and taut. "Cathy, get her out. Immediately."

This was my mother's cue to walk Jane to the living room, to switch channels on the TV and leave it on the first animated animal face she saw and turn up the volume. And then you were alone in the room with my father. I assume you went over the basics then, as you'd been trained to do: medical history, initial nature of the complaint, just like you were doing rounds. He must have disclosed the intestinal distress that kept him in the bathroom for a good portion of every day. Then the appointment with the gastroenterologist, a series of humiliating tests to rule out cancer and ulcers and other things, the diagnosis of inflammatory bowel disease, and the prescription for a nonsteroidal anti-inflammatory. It was at this point, I'm sure, that you were chomping at the bit to finish his sentences, in the full flush of your shining hour. You were an intern, your brain still overeager to stuff itself with every maverick case study and miraculous exception that ever existed, every medically neglected phenomenon. And this one was disgracefully underdiagnosed; everyone forgot about it because it was such an obvious answer. But you must have seen it somewhere—a photo of an anonymous flayed body in a textbook and under it a caption: two of the most common and colorless surnames in the English language, united by a hyphen. I always imagined you pumping a finger in the air, triumphant as Jonas Salk: "Voilà! Stevens-Johnson syndrome!" But I know the whole thing was probably anticlimactic. You must have told him to stop taking the medication, that he was having a reaction, a reaction so severe it merited proper-noun status. Get your liver checked, you would have told him. He would have been meek and appreciative. Then—and this I know on good authority—my mother was summoned and kept crying, thanking you over and over and saying, "We didn't know what to do. We thought he was dying." According to Jane, my father croaked out, "Don't say that! We did not! That's bullshit." He continued yelling at her after you left. Jane told me.

As far as you're concerned, the story ends here. He did what you said. He got better, he went on to live a productive life with no lingering ill effects, and he is still alive, retired, reading Stephen Hawking and Carl Sagan, eating Raisin Bran, and monitoring his cholesterol in a Grass Valley, California, bungalow, with my mother and an ancient cat and two German shepherds. But there is more to it than this. Few people have the luxury of knowing the impact of their coincidental gestures—how being in the right place at the right time fixes them in some stranger's memory, a signpost marking a fork in the road: this changed everything. I bet there are a lot of people who think of you that way. You've probably saved a lot of lives and helped mitigate the pain of countless others. Maybe this is just another testimonial to add to the pile; or maybe my father was your signpost, and you've been haunted by him all these years, that desecrated pile of flesh issuing civilities, the voice box in that charred husk, and the surprising simplicity of the save.

The only connections that retain their integrity are the forever unconsummated. So call this a consummation, because I like to ruin things. Here is what happened after you saved his life and left. In a nutshell: He got better, I got older, and I grew to resent his presence in my life. From the time of my earliest memories, I wanted him gone. Not necessarily dead, but gone. Vanished.

A couple months after you saved his life, the tornado came. The chances of a tornado striking a downtown metropolitan area were one in five hundred. Five patients in a million developed Stevens-Johnson from nonsteroidal meds. In the extraordinary second half of 1980 my father encountered both phenomena and lived.

Five people died. Seventy were hospitalized. The roof of Jane's elementary school caved in and the downtown streets were strewn with pink insulation and the detritus of commerce: bank deposit slips and receipts, memos, pages from ledgers, restaurant menus. It also destroyed the animal research wing of Bingham, where the toads and monkeys and cats were kept before being dispatched to the departments that needed them. My father, as you may recall, worked in the basement nephrology lab doing something with the single-celled bladders of Dominican toads. I know that they were killed in the disaster but in my mind I see them as unkillable by any force of nature beyond my father and his shiny, sharp, and painless pith. *Bufo marinus* toads in the wild are born out of mud and melt back into mud when they die. Their life cycles are only one year, and primitive peoples, upon seeing one large bumpy body sink into the mud and an identical one come back out, thought the toads were magical creatures that could rise from the dead. I cannot help but imagine them hopping through the wreckage of the city in the wake of the twister, disappearing into swampy banks of the Kalamazoo River and, in summer, when my father was recovered and we had our power back,

emerging again—all the ugly bodies with their humanlike
bladders and their potential for unlocking the secrets of equi-
librium—from the mud of each backyard.

The toads were my father's closest companions for fifteen
years. Fifty hours a week, five floors below the surgical wing
where you did your rounds, he was alone with them. He even
made a mascot of one of the fattest, turned it into a joke with
the lab techs, named it Fritz and vowed never to kill it. He
kept a photograph of Fritz on his desk at home. Fritz and his
ilk were brownish green, the size of two men's fists side by
side, with morbid shiny eyes and poisonous white secretions
oozing from their sebaceous glands, squirming and alive, but
not for long. My father was always careful to point out that
they felt no pain. "I do not enjoy killing," he would tell us,
and describe how quickly it was done: how he'd carry the toad
to the counter and bend its head down with one latex-gloved
finger and slide the pith into its neck, severing the spinal cord.
What he wanted was its bladder: a swatch of slimy lucidity
inside the horny helmet of the toad's skin. He hated the job,
really: alone in the porous granite cell of the lab all day for
fifteen years straight, coming home at night terrified of whatever contaminants still clung to his clothes. Regardless, his
work paved the way for half the surgeries you and your colleagues performed and ever will perform.

He could have been a doctor. He was smart enough. In
adolescence I nursed an irrational rage at him for not sticking
it out and becoming a doctor. I thought we could have been
rich. Private schools, nice clothes, a father who didn't exhibit
the psychological effects of having spent fifteen years alone in
a basement with the knowledge that his family's livelihood

depended solely on year-to-year government grants and his
ability to prove this work was worth it, was producing results,
he and the toads pleading their case before disembodied
bureaucrats year after year. Was it any wonder he had inflammatory bowels?

He was a nervous man. But even though he was still weak
when the tornado hit, still convalescing, it did not unnerve
him. It decimated part of the neighborhood, but our block—
the block we shared with you—was relatively untouched. The
windows of our back porch shattered. I remember the sky
turned a glaring coppery green, and the cartoon rabbit on the
TV screen warped and twisted, replaced by a grainy Weather
Alert. Then the warning siren. My mother was good about
bustling the two of us downstairs in a cheery no-nonsense
manner. My father picked up the dog and followed us down,
issuing orders not to go upstairs for any reason.

But as soon as we were settled, he stole up the stairs. He
wanted to see the funnel cloud. This is something I still marvel
at—my father, a man who had never been drunk or done
drugs or anything stupidly adventurous in his life, a man who
warned of the dangers of gum-chewing and mandated that we
use at least six sheets of Kleenex for each nose-blowing, going
up the stairs into the eye of a natural disaster. It may have been
his one and only chance to see a funnel cloud. To think of
who he was when he was alone, absolutely alone, face exultant
with concentration as he stared out the big living room picture
window and watched a dervish of dust, connected like an
umbilical cord to the mass of cloud above it, materialize in the
air and dip down every so often with a terrifyingly purposeful
illusion of precision, to think of our house given a pass as

though smeared with lamb's blood, and him watching as the funnel disappeared on the horizon, is to think of him as an absolute stranger.

I've seen that cloud since. A tornado is the only natural disaster that never gets named—no Katrina, no Loma Prieta, no Vesuvius—and so it's easy to suspend disbelief and tell myself that the same cloud appears on the horizon over and over, just smaller or larger, the duration of its siege lengthening or shortening according to factors unknown. It's a thousand serpents twining, a conical head of Medusa but sleeker, more compressed, centrifugal and furious, its appetite for destruction tinged with cruel whimsy: it can pick up a grown man and hold him in midair for a while—as if for some vigil, some examination—and then return him hours later and miles away, dead, unscathed but missing his shoes and socks. It plays tricks. It's like those rare moments in life when we are hit with an urge to explain. Along with the delusion that everyone cares, that everyone has been waiting with bated breath all along, all through the long desert of our silence, and after we tell all they will look at us with dewy pride and love. Every time it's the same. Every outpouring reorders the world for a few terrifying seconds but ultimately leaves it stoically unchanged; every speech is the same, a big screaming dervish with a hole in the center, and we know this but we still believe this one will be different, we weren't telling the right things before but this time we will, this is the big one, the real one, the one that needs to be heard.

So we draw in our breath.

Then we realize the siren is gone and so is the danger. But we keep explaining.

I will never know what it is to save a person's life. And you, Doctor, will never know what it is to be a man's daughter.

On paper, he was an excellent father. He read to us, took us to Disney World, initiated board games and basketball, didn't beat or molest us, was conscientious to a fault about keeping us fed and clothed and healthy. But he never treated us like children. If we crossed him, he retaliated, less like an adult scolding a child than a ship captain berating a duplicitous subordinate whose treachery put the whole vessel at risk. He was convinced we were betraying him, all of us, even our mother, who struggled to preempt his tantrums and did not protect me when I tried to defend her. There was a tacit agreement that he was owed something, and justified in any method of extracting his due.

"Filled with hate," he'd say, shaking his head. "Just filled with disrespect and ugliness and hate." And do you know what the worst part was? He could never bring himself to do anything. When he threatened to beat me with a belt, I knew not to take him seriously. It was impossible to imagine him doing something as ritualized and prolonged, as quaintly disciplinary, as administering corporal punishment. There is an element of faith in such a practice, an earnest investment in orderliness and cause-and-effect, a naïve reaffirmation of parent-child roles that would have belied his belief that I, and not he, was the villain of our household. And it would entail actually touching me.

The "abuse" was so ridiculous—the pronouncements, the grandiose Shakespearean threats, the melodrama—that whatever pain or fear I may have felt was bleached out in retrospect, and I have come to believe that my past itself is ridiculous. It is doubly ridiculous to claim to be damaged by such absurdities. It is akin to being molested by a man in a Goofy suit at Disney World: the ludicrous aspect invalidates the traumatic. For the benefit of friends and lovers, I have considered translating past events into something less out-landishly dysfunctional, like a divorce, or a philandering parent or an alcoholic one or a shiftless no-good charming one, or, yes, an early and conventional death—misfortunes other people understand. And this is where you come in. If it weren't for you, there would be nothing to tell beyond "He died when I was four." I would be fucked up the way people are supposed to be fucked up: without a whiff of the macabre.

And how, you may ask, does this profound and irreparable damage manifest? Am I a shut-in? An underachiever? On the contrary: I got my bachelor's and my master's. I am a court advocate for foster children and victims of domestic battery. When I tell people this their faces soften with vague guilt and they refrain from telling off-color jokes in my presence, or any jokes at all. What they say is, "You must be a very com-passionate person." What they mean is, "You must have been a raped and battered foster child." In front of the judge's dais, I find myself channeling my father: the exhaustive exac-titude of his phrasing, his clinical mastery and his dainty manipulation of elegant, audibly punctuated clauses; and the judges look at me the way I imagine legions of doctors have looked at him as he stood in their offices pitching a drug that stops people from wetting themselves and describing it in a way that made it sound like the most dignified product in the world.

Ten years after you saved his life, he left the toads for good. Bingham closed down the lab and left him jobless at forty-six. He was out of work for a year before getting an entry-level sales job with a pharmaceutical company. He stayed in the basement until dawn every night, mastering the intricacies of each drug, practicing his approach in the mirror and with my mother playing the role of doctor, relearning how to talk to people, until he achieved the highest sales numbers in the district and eventually the state.

He kept the photo of Fritz next to a human kidney in a jar of formaldehyde on his desk. He took the kidney with him after the lab closed. Pink and buoyant, it drifted in the cloudy liquid like a shrimp in soup stock. When I was fourteen I asked him whose kidney it was. He wouldn't tell me. In his defense, I had asked in an archly derisive manner that implied there was something perverse about keeping an internal organ in a jar on a desk.

Ten years later, when I was eighteen weeks' pregnant with my first son, the fuzzy pulsating shape on the ultrasound screen reminded me of nothing so much as that kidney: the bulbous head curled protectively, fetally, over the tapered end with the compact integrity of a grub, so dense with function, a reptilian triumph of function and design. My husband and the ultrasound technician thought I was crying because of the overwhelming joy of seeing the fetus for the first time, and maybe I was, but there was something else that I couldn't explain, sitting up and staring, slime smeared on my belly as the scanner, like a computer mouse or a Ouija board's planchette, roved in slow circles over it. There was something terribly vulnerable about that doubled-over posture, something that spoke of a dutiful unsentimentality of instinct, like a turtle with its head retracted or a rabbit frozen, head tucked, in the grass as a hawk flies over.

Shortly thereafter I called my father and asked him again whose kidney it was. Although taken aback, he humored me: he loved explaining medical phenomena. He told me the kidney was taken from a cadaver. "Someone who died too suddenly for any of the organs to be harvested," he said. "So the surgeons parceled them out for research departments to use as anatomical models." He described where the kidneys are in the body, clinging like tree frogs to the cord of the ureter. I asked him why he kept it for so long. He said, without hesitation, "Because I didn't want it to be thrown away."

My father and I talk on the phone semi-frequently these days. He and my mother adopted an old white cat from a shelter who reminds him, he says, of me. "She's aloof," he said, "and she prefers to be alone. But she's so gentle." On birthdays, I get two cards: one from my parents and another ostensibly from the cat, signed in a wavery, unsteady script. My husband finds this hilarious. So do I. This is the side of him they see: my husband and our two sons. I have finally realized that this is his only side, and that the one I knew before is gone. And I'm glad that my husband and children know him as this. I am glad they will never see his tomato-red face and scrawled brows, the opaque and terrifying flatness dropping over his eyes like an extra set of lids. I'm glad they will never cringe at the clink of car keys dropping into a metal Folgers can: the sound that meant he was home from work. And at the same time I am not glad at all.

There is a bitterness that wants validation. There is a need for recompense, for recognition. There is an anger that will never see consummation. My husband will never know that I am able to love him despite having vowed at the age of five that I would never marry or even let a man come near me, that love is weak, that it depreciates in value as soon as you give yourself up. Sometimes I look at the man I married—the temperate mildness of him, the scrunchy innocence of his yawns—and I am inconsolably, furiously lonely.

"I see what you and your father have in common," he said after meeting my family for the first time. I waited. He went on, "It's the way you use words. You both pick your words like you're stripping dead buds off a houseplant, but with this strange exhilaration. This fastidious, fussy exhilaration." He shook his head and looked at me, exultant. "It's exactly the same."

Telling him would corrupt something, some tentative, delicate, beautiful thing. And I am so glad that he loves my father; I want so badly for my father to be surrounded by love, by as many people's love as possible, and for all this love to give him everything he wants so he won't ever feel alone. And I feel this terrible pity for both of them, my father and my husband: in my mind, I see them navigating their way in the world, unwitting, before the power I choose not to wield.

My father once showed me a picture in his junior high yearbook: a group shot of the J.V. basketball team. He was the only one wearing clunky black dress shoes with his uniform, having offered his sneakers to the team's best, albeit most forgetful, player. He knelt in the front row with one shiny oxford foremost, lean and soft-eyed, his expression strangely adult in its staunch readiness to graciously acquiesce. His teammates'

faces were vacant and surly. Many years later, en route to dropping me off at college, he exploded at the possibility—casually
broached by my mother—that my as-yet-unseen roommate
might have taken "the better bed."

"Why are *we* always the ones who have to compromise?"
he raged. "I'm sick of it! Why do *we* always get the short end
of the stick?"

After they hugged me goodbye and left me with my dorm
adviser and the six strangers who were to be my floormates, I
looked around at the blue carpet, the high peaked ceilings,
the windows with their view of a grassy quad—everything I
had looked forward to—and I wept. I had never cried so
much or for so long. I was mortified. "Do you miss your parents?" my new roommate asked sweetly, and I nodded, but I
knew that wasn't really it. Or at least wasn't all of it. My sudden distress felt limbic, hunted, guilty, inextricably tied to my
father watching a tornado demolish the city; my father fram-
ing a photograph of a fat toad; lying in bed and insisting, like
an irascible monarch with no suitable heirs, that he was not
dying. In every mental snapshot his face bore one expression:
the strange exhilaration of a bemused witness to the vagaries
of the world. I thought of how often I'd wished him gone.
And the act of leaving home, beginning a life in which he was
not a primary player, an irritant and adversary, a dense saturat-
ing presence, felt like a betrayal—not only of him, but of
myself. Left with a father who existed only in bite-sized frag-
ments, phone conversations, secondhand anecdotes, I could
no longer fear him because he was no longer my father. I had
no choice but to love him. And I mourned it—the loss of that
insulating resistance—like a death.

And I have mourned it ever since. Any display of vulnerability on his part—cleaning a spot off his bifocals, misunder-
standing a gas station attendant's directions—can move me to
furious tears. On visits home Jane and I can't stop peppering
him with stupid questions—"Dad, do cats have lips? Do they
have eyelashes?"—and we fall all over each other as he says,
"The question is not whether cats have eyelashes, but why
anyone in their right mind would care," playing the role of
humorless scientist because he knows we find it funny. When
I talk to him on the phone he ends by saying, "I love you,"
with a certain tentative determination. When I don't say it
back enthusiastically enough, or if we've been arguing, he says,
"Are you sure?" He tends to mug when expressing positive
emotions, exaggeratedly modeling each sentiment as though
reading to children from a storybook.

He tried to overcome his skinniness in high school by eating
five sandwiches for lunch every day. He distrusted his long
eyelashes and the Byronic pensiveness of his face. His features,
untouched by illness, were those of a matinee idol crossed with
a puppy: a blend of dumb entreaty and consumptive melan-
choly, made even stranger by the affable sweetness of his public self, the eagerness to ingratiate, the smart sincerity that made
him an excellent salesman. Doctors—like you—trusted and
respected him. He could talk to them on their level. And at the
same time do the two-handed handshake, haul in the trays of
bagels and fruit, the boxes of samples that clogged our garage
for years along with the pens and night-lights and mugs and
T-shirts emblazoned with the names of antidepressants and
painkillers. Doctors treated him with the doting jocularity of
high school jocks toward the smart kid who does their home-

work for a fee. Why do I want so badly for you to understand what you saved?

And what, in so doing, you gave me: a life sentence of uneasy love for a man I used to fear. I hope I can write a good eulogy. I hope I can forgive myself for every dark wish I ever had. I hope that, secretly, he never really loved me. I hope I die before he does. I hope I never have to see him suffer. And I hope that someday I can say thank you for saving him and thank you for disappearing and thank you for not responding with a letter saying you remember that day in great detail and pointing out all the things I got wrong. Every person who lives a life eventually starts to make it all up: not just the past but the future, too. The only thing you can't create is the present, while it's happening—you going about your day, Doctor, not knowing what I'm thinking, and God knows where you are: you could be saving someone, you could be killing someone, you could be breaking the news of a death, you could be filling out charts, or you could be slicing a person open as they sleep, skin flaps pulled back like pages in a book, your silver hummingbird dipping into a dark mass of pomegranate-red tissue and coming back out, that simple, that improbably facile, and depositing in a crescent-shaped silver basin the pulpy lethal bit that doesn't belong. I'd want it sealed in a jar and given to me: the thing that necessitated such an opening.

Once the white cat got lost. My father made flyers, called neighbors, canvassed the streets. After three days my mother said the cat was surely dead. But on the fourth day it occurred to my father to look under the backyard deck. At first he mistook her for a wadded-up towel. But then he saw her eyes glowing in the dark. She greeted him with a pained, relieved rasp.

It is a story he likes to tell.

"She was waiting for me to find her," he says. His voice is marveling, humble. "She walked right into my arms!"

none of the above

When she first began teaching, Alma promised herself she would never wear a sweater with an apple on it. In her most uncompromising moods, appliqués were altogether banned. There were other things she swore never to do: talk about her husband in front of the class; praise her girl students for docility and her boy students for assertiveness; shake her index finger at anyone; and, most of all, hesitate to act immediately at the slightest sign of child abuse. In two years of teaching the third grade, the apple veto was the only vow she managed to keep.

She saw the red puncture mark on Peter Grissom's wrist during a tornado drill, as she walked around making sure the kids were crouching under their desks and holding hardcover texts over their heads as ordered. It was the second month of the new school year. The flesh surrounding the mark on Peter's

wrist was bright as Kool-Aid. The other children giggled and
kicked one another and let their books slide off. Only Peter
stared ahead, centering *Science and You* over the crown of his
head, waiting for the drill to end with the preternatural, frozen
patience of something in camouflage: a soldier, or an animal.

"If that was a real tornado," she told the kids afterward,
"you all would have died."

A few of them laughed. She blurted out, "It's not funny!"

All semester she'd been watching Peter. Before the puncture
there'd been other marks, shallow but troubling, and occasional
scratches. Something about this boy made her feel transparent
and compromised, the way she sometimes felt walking past an
angry-looking handicapped person on the street. This feeling
was underscored by the way Peter, his arms and hands streaked
with red swaths as if a dozen Band-Aids had been ripped off at
once, looked at her—not shamefacedly, but with a prickly,
practiced flash of irritated awareness, as if he knew exactly what
she was looking at and could foresee the conclusions she would
draw at home later that night in the kitchen with her husband,
her black skirt and conservative blouse exchanged for pink
terrycloth loungewear, saying, *I might have a case of child abuse on
my hands,* in that deferent tone of implied appeal she always
slipped into when talking to her husband about school, whether
he was listening or not, whether she needed his advice or not.
Usually she didn't. She just got sick of talking in her teacher
voice, that pleasantly instructive drone with its half-ironic edge
of threat. She began to feel like a sock puppet in a morning-
show revue: diabolically singsongy in the most incongruous
circumstances, vocal cords eternally tuned to the cadences of
"If You're Happy and You Know It."

Peter always joined in when she led the class in that song or any other. "Who Put the Overalls in Mrs. Murphy's Chowder?"; "The Hokey Pokey"; "Farmer in the Dell." He participated in Heads Up 7-Up. He could spell. His aptitude scores were above average. He did nothing disturbing with building blocks, action figures. For a while she organized arts-and-crafts activities in the half-conscious hope that he would unwittingly betray himself through a nonverbal medium: finger painting, paper-bag masks, finger puppets, family portraits in crayon. But he drew sunny skies and houses with smoking chimneys and large striped animals frolicking on the lawn. Alma knew the signs. Abused and neglected children were (a) withdrawn; (b) developmentally delayed; or (c) "acting out," a term she despised for its jargony inexactitude, but she knew it when she saw it. And Peter was none of the above.

The day of the tornado drill, she came home to find Kurt, her husband, hunched in his ergonomic swivel chair, a cup of coffee on his mouse pad. He worked from home as a freelance graphic designer.

"Hey," he'd always say to her, without turning around. "Did you show those kids who's boss?"

On good days, Alma responded breezily. On bad days— when she'd written twelve boys' names on the board and they still hadn't stopped calling out, "Penis!" at ten-second intervals, when she lost her temper and her voice broke, when she had to call some kid's parents and tell them that their child had a learning disability or a speech impediment or was bullying some other child—it took self-restraint not to snap at Kurt, not to take his jovial daily icebreaker as a covert indictment. But on the day of the tornado drill, the day she saw the puncture mark on Peter's wrist, she put down her satchel and took off her coat and, when Kurt grinned over his shoulder and said, "So? Did you whip those little bastards into shape?" she winced on his behalf and said, "I might have a case of child abuse on my hands."

If only he had a black eye. Or a limp. Then, she told Kurt, it would be easy to take action. But Peter's injuries were not concomitant with the use of force.

Kurt reminded her that this was Beulah, Michigan, population eight thousand, where the lopsided ratio of wildlife to humans resulted in newsworthy freak accidents of escalating bizarreness. "Remember the raccoon?" he said.

Alma did remember the raccoon. It happened the first winter she and Kurt moved from Ann Arbor to Beulah. A forty-something man and his eighteen-year-old child bride lived with their toddler girl in a pole barn. They kept raccoons as pets. One morning, the parents awoke to find half their baby's face eaten off. When relaying this incident to noninhabitants— her mother and brother and grad school friends—Alma forced herself to speak in an anchorwoman monotone one octave lower than normal, stripped of all her usual storytelling mannerisms, in order to keep from veering into helpless and hideously inappropriate laughter.

"What are you *doing* there?" her mother asked from the manicured quadrangles of the University of Michigan, where she held a Distinguished Chair in women's studies. Her prim horror put Alma in mind of the pearl-clutching mothers of enterprising pioneers, shades of Pa Ingalls's disapproving urban in-laws. Alma changed the subject, partly due to sudden shame at the realization that her literary allusions were confined to juvenilia.

So it could be a feral animal, she conceded. Or it could be the natural by-product of rural living. Boys, she had been told, were always scraping themselves up. Alma had embarrassed herself her first year by calling Steve Tucker's mother to say she'd noticed "abrasions" on his hands. There was a silence. Then Mrs. Tucker said, "Well, he's been helping his dad get rid of briars and wasps' nests all summer. That's bound to cause a few . . . what was the word you used? Abrasions."

Alma must have sounded surprised, because Mrs. Tucker added, not unkindly but with authoritative flatness, "Boys around here work. They get scraped up from time to time."

And as tempted as she was to dismiss Mrs. Tucker as a back-woods Ma Kettle with a lip full of snuff, Alma couldn't help but recognize the woman's certainty in what she knew to be true, her lack of passive aggression in relaying it, the brisk civility underlying her bluntness. Alma herself could have used some of that. She assumed that in a few years she would start to take it on, the flinty assurance of the veteran instructors—Beulah mothers all—along with their insulating asexuality. For now, though, she was an anomaly; the little girls in her class tended to love her because she was young and wore makeup and looked like a softer approximation of the women they saw on TV: blond, with breasts. You didn't have to be especially pretty or thin for little girls to admire you, she'd discovered. You just had to exhibit a few qualities—a contoured waist, a shiny red manicure, demonstrated aptitude with a large-barreled curling iron—that they associated, albeit unconsciously, with a certain ritualistic female mystique their own mothers had no time for.

Alma could remember how mesmerized she'd been as a seven-year-old by a billboard she passed every day on her way to school in Ann Arbor: an ivory-skinned, voluptuous cartoon woman in a lavender teddy, lounging and smiling, with a speech balloon attached to her candy-apple mouth that said *COME VISIT THE VELVET TOUCH.* She had begged her mother to take her to the Velvet Touch—a dumpy one-story brick building painted purple—on a daily basis and her mother had uncomfortably demurred, one day finally reaching her breaking point and snapping, "Alma, that is a *sex store!* That is a store where they sell *pornography!*" But that was what little girls loved: the cheap gleam of effort. At the end of each year, at least five or six of them would give her a present with a handwritten note along the lines of *YOU'RE MY FAVRIT TEACHER* or *YOUR SO PRETTY I'LL MISS YOU.*

The boys were not so easily won over. When she yelled, it was usually at them. A few made sniggering jokes about her breasts in her hearing, without even knowing what was so funny—they just knew, from their fathers or older brothers, that the larger a woman's breasts the more ridiculous her pretense at authority, that a large-breasted woman telling you what to do might as well be wearing a red clown's nose or Groucho glasses. As the faculty's only woman of childbearing age, Alma never brought this problem up in staff meetings. She never even told Kurt. It was the boys, always the boys. And it occurred to her that her hesitation to investigate Peter's injuries had less to do with her own embarrassment and more to do with the fact that *he* was a boy, a particularly unnerving boy, a boy who did everything she told him to do with the self-contained bemusement of a good sport.

Nothing about him was childlike. His sawdust–colored hair was clearly kept short by some adult with a sharp pair of scissors, but he never showed up scalped and skulking beneath the blunt, squarish contours of an obvious new haircut, unlike the others with their bowl cuts or buzzed domes or classic choirboy mops with shaved and tapered undersides. Peter's hair looked like it just grew that way, short in the back and longer in the front, with his ears peeking elfishly behind wispy sideburns. He was a sturdy boy but not stout, with a smooth face and long-lashed hazel eyes and a couple of raised beauty marks at the outer corner of one eye. The placement and double symmetry of the beauty marks gave his face an overfinished and doll-like quality, but were also sensually, immoderately fleshly in a way that made Alma slightly uncomfortable. He was not one of the breast commentators. But he sat in his chair like a man—a khaki-pants-and-braided-belt-wearing, slightly nerdy man, akin to the guys she'd known in grad school—slouched on his tailbone with his legs apart, tapping a pencil in the air, like a wunderkind leaning back in a swivel chair in the loft space of some Internet start-up company. Alma once saw him pick up a crayon that had rolled off Lisa Schull's desk and, with a perfunctory and businesslike gesture, put it back so unobtrusively that Lisa didn't even notice. During tests, he cupped and rubbed his chin with his mouth firmly downturned, like someone's dad reading the newspaper.

It made her wonder about Peter's dad. She looked up his name in the class directory—Russell Grissom—and tried to recall if she'd ever been told his profession. The Beulah fathers who weren't farmers were usually contractors, maintenance men, owners of local franchises and family businesses, landscapers, park rangers, technicians of some sort, men who wore uniforms or goggles, had spatial intelligence, did nothing effetely creative or liberal-artsy: no ad executives or copywriters or academics or journalists or designers. She used this basis to create an internal picture of Russell Grissom, one she revisited with each new scratch and scuff. He was, she envisioned, a man governed by a primitive, reactive notion of discipline. Not a martinet—too hasty and inconsistent for that, too enamored of shortcuts. From the haphazard nature of Peter's injuries and his air of controlled, incurious wariness, she imagined his paterfamilias as an unreflective oaf who simply wanted his son out of his hair, who wasn't above tying the child to a chair if he caught him messing around with his toolbox or the stove, a man motivated not by premeditated sadism but a lazy dependence on short-term solutions. In order to be hurt by him, you had to be in the wrong place at the wrong time. It was a credit to Peter's resourcefulness that he had not been hurt worse.

At the first parent-teacher conference in November, Alma hung the classroom with the children's construction-paper turkeys and harvest horns and assembled a student portfolio for each set of parents. The conferences went smoothly. All night Alma sat at her desk in her brown corduroy pants—the kind her mother would approvingly call "slacks"—and the chunky espresso cardigan that obscured her chest, hair in a wooden barrette. She was autumnal, desexed, operating on autopilot while a tensed, alert part of her held back, waiting and waiting for the Grissoms. Both parents had RSVP'd yes.

When they finally showed up—at eight p.m., a half hour before the evening was supposed to end—she didn't realize it was them until the tall woman in the red windbreaker strode ahead of her husband and extended her hand to Alma, smiled broadly with big white Kennedy-esque teeth—the teeth of a debutante-turned-equestrienne—and said, "So sorry we're late, Mrs. Quinn. How annoying, right? I'm glad you're still here. We belong to Peter."

Mrs. Grissom said this with a certain jaunty self-effacement, as if in ironic concession to the fact that her son, although absent, took center stage in this setting. Next to her, Mr. Grissom roused himself to action, smiling and shaking Alma's hand. He was three inches shorter than his wife.

Alma stood and fumbled around for Peter's portfolio.

"I'm so glad you came," she said. "Peter is—he's a great kid."

This was what she said about everyone's kid. But Mrs. Grissom, taking her seat across from Alma's big desk, widened her eyes and tilted her head. "Oh, I'm so glad," she said. She spoke as if vehemently brushing something aside.

Mr. Grissom spoke at last.

"Peter's an only child," he blurted. Then he grimaced a little, as if this implied failure on his part. "So we're always a little concerned about his socialization. But if he's getting along with the other kids—"

"Oh, yes," Alma said. "Definitely. Peter gets along just fine with the others."

This wasn't a lie. Peter *did* get along fine with the others. He got along with them the way a tiny bird gets along with the hippopotamus it happens to alight on: with sublime and blithe indifference.

She handed the Grissoms Peter's portfolio. She had encouraged the children to decorate their covers, and they'd obediently drawn stars and rainbows and dogs and rockets and flowers and lightning bolts around their names. Except for Peter, who had merely written his full name—Peter Edward Grissom—in black Sharpie in the upper left corner, as if drafting a memo.

"Don't you want to make it a little more colorful than that?" Alma asked him. "This is to show your parents on conference day."

And Peter half smiled at her, picked up his Sharpie again, and said, "Sure."

Now she saw that the only augmentation he'd made was a bold, ruler-straight black border around the perimeter of the paper, its edges slightly fluted. His name still soberly occupied the upper corner. The whole thing was in distressingly good taste. It looked like a law firm's letterhead.

"No words wasted," Mr. Grissom said. He spoke about Peter in a tone of matter-of-fact marveling, in contrast to his wife's warbling, slightly vinegary indulgence. In fact he sounded almost awed.

He didn't look like Peter. He was short and slight, with messy dark hair. When Alma spoke, he leaned toward her intently, his upper body inclined in a deferential arc, as though lowering a drawbridge for her words to walk across. His brow kept wrinkling in a flinching, preemptive way; it looked to Alma as if he expected her to start speaking in tongues, and was less worried about not understanding her than about *appearing* not to understand her. He had none of Peter's dusky golden inscrutability.

Mrs. Grissom—"Call me Tyler," she'd said firmly, but Alma, for some reason, could not—didn't look like Peter, either. In conversation she was just as attentive as her husband, but in a different way. She affirmed Alma's points by nodding and saying, "Gotcha!" with a snatchy, satisfied air of acquisition, like a bidder at an auction. When it became apparent that Mrs. Grissom was making preparations to escape—tightly tying off her sentences at the ends, like balloons—Alma leaped, panicked, for her chance.

"There's one last thing," she said. She smiled so they wouldn't get alarmed. "It's just something I've been noticing about Peter."

"Sure," Mrs. Grissom said. Mr. Grissom was almost completely horizontal.

Alma took a breath. "I've noticed—Peter sometimes comes in with these scratches on his body. And then once in a while he'll show up with these other marks—almost like puncture marks?"

For a second, both Grissoms' faces went completely blank, stunned, as if reeling from a sudden strobe of blinding light. Then they recovered. Mr. Grissom looked down, and his wife's face regained its arch, fey opacity. Alma kept waiting for them to look at one another. They didn't.

Finally Mrs. Grissom said, "Oh, boy. We really need to start putting our foot down."

Alma waited. Mrs. Grissom sighed and turned toward her. Her body language was conciliatory, but when she spoke, the declarative momentum of her voice did not flag.

"Peter *loves* tools," she said. "I think he's going to grow up to be an engineer or something. He fiddles with things—my alarm clock, the table lamps, he wants to know how things work, you know? So we try to nurture that. We got him his own tool chest."

"But he prefers mine," her husband cut in, grinning.

Mrs. Grissom nodded approvingly at him. "Oh, yes, he does. If it can explode, if it can stab him in the eye, you can't keep it away from him. And I see him all banged up, and I come at him—let me at those scrapes, I say—but Peter doesn't want any part of it." She shrugged her shoulders up to her ears, palms facing up. "I think he takes pride in it, actually. Thinks it's manly."

"Workman's comp," interjected Mr. Grissom. Even though this made no sense, his wife laughed and said, "Uh-huh. You got it."

Alma wondered if Mrs. Grissom had even heard what her husband had said before reflexively affirming it. And this was the point when she knew that she did not believe them.

"Okay," she said. She was ready for the conference to be over. "Well, maybe there's some way to supervise him when he's playing. Whether he likes it or not."

"Oh, definitely," Mrs. Grissom said. "Absolutely."

There was a silence. Alma looked from one parent to the other, and for a moment she felt like *she* was their child, wary, on the lookout for anything that made sense, grasping for some pattern of predictability to guide her through the maze of their world. A surge of grief lashed through her. She didn't know if it was for Peter, or for his parents—so pitiable suddenly in their shameful haste to escape—or for herself, trapped in this cheerful room with two people she knew were lying, every nerve and synapse in her body rebelling against what she would have to do tomorrow, the conversation she would have to initiate, face to face, with this lying couple's sphinxlike, mysteriously mauled son.

———

Alma waited until everyone had finished their milk and eaten lunch. As the class shuffled outside for recess she snagged Peter's sleeve and said, "Peter? Can you hang on a second?"

He was sporting an extra-large waterproof Band-Aid on his left cheekbone. He looked at her like a restaurant patron politely waiting out the server's tedious recitation of specials before placing his order.

Alma smiled at him. "Peter," she said, "I've noticed you've been coming in with a lot of scratches and marks on your skin."

She paused. He kept looking at her. There was something odd about his poise, a vacancy to it; she wondered if he was disassociating. She'd read the literature on trauma and detachment.

"Can you tell me how they got there?" she said.

Peter blinked and straightened in his chair.

"I don't know," he said. "I play soccer. We go camping and stuff. I don't know."

He was smiling at her: affable, composed.

Alma pressed on. Her gaze kept straying to the scratched-raw hands extending from the cuffs of his black-and-red plaid wool jacket, folded on his lap.

"Okay," she said, "but you don't get scratched up like that in soccer. Or hiking. And sometimes it looks worse than a scratch—more like a gash, a deeper cut. Are you sure that's from sports?"

Peter shrugged. "I play basketball, too."

Alma thought, *Screw it.* "Peter," she said, "look at your hands right now. You're going to tell me that's from basketball?"

Peter stared at his hands.

Alma made her voice as sweet and soft as possible.

"Peter," she said, "all you have to do is tell me the truth. You're not going to get in trouble just for telling the truth."

He was silent for a moment longer. Alma felt virtuous and sick. Then Peter raised his head and looked at her: resolute, unashamed, with the slightest glint of craftiness in his eyes.

"All right," he said. He leaned forward.

And Alma suddenly didn't want to know. She wanted to backtrack, to say, *Okay, basketball, bow-hunting, whatever.* She wanted to be wrong, too misguidedly wrong to ever live it down. Wrong enough for public shame. For firing.

But she didn't cover her ears. She sat there and trained her practiced, tempered gaze on Peter as he looked her in the eye and informed her, without preamble or disclaimer, that he'd been attacked by a tiger.

Actually he never used the word *attack.*

"I have a pet tiger cub at home," he said. "He sleeps in my bed with me. Sometimes when I play with him he'll scratch. Or bite. He doesn't mean to, though. It's not a big deal."

She waited. He kept talking.

"He's just a baby," he said. His voice was fondly permissive. "He's a Bengal tiger. From India. There are only five hundred left in the wild. And I'm going to raise him until he's full-grown and then put him in a wildlife preserve so he can run free. Because my parents say he'll be too expensive to feed once he's big."

He smiled at her.

Alma looked into the boy's tawny, unreadable face and for one horrible moment she could barely restrain herself from slapping him. He was fucking with her now. Was this what his parents told him to say? *The whole family,* she said to herself, *the whole family's psychotic.*

Then Peter reached up and rubbed the inner corner of one eye. He looked exhausted, as if he'd been staying up nights. The Band-Aid on his face was edged with grime, and she could see the tiny dense hairs of his cheeks mashed and gummed with adhesive. Right then, he looked so much like a little boy that she almost cried. Then she remembered that he actually was one.

"Peter," she said. "Is that really what you want to tell me? That you sleep with a tiger?"

Peter smirked at her knowingly, as if some nascent part of him were on Alma's side and could appreciate, on a hypothetical level, the inconvenience of dealing with this bizarre and stubborn child.

"It's not what I *want* to tell you," he said. "It's just a fact."

When Alma first started teaching, it permeated every facet of her life. She imagined that the kids could see every move she made, in and out of the classroom. She felt an obligation to keep her face neutrally pleasant while washing the dishes, shaving her legs, changing a tampon, using the toilet. She couldn't have sex with Kurt; it felt perverse to try and do that with the neutrally pleasant expression on her face, as if she were one of those insipidly smiling, pliable bimbos in old *Playboy* cartoons, with their bovine air of complacent and remote satiation. She was ashamed. She kept thinking of the phrase *stupid cow.* They saw a couples counselor thirty miles away in Marquette. The counselor gave Alma and Kurt an assignment: never talk about work—or anything peripherally related to work—in the bedroom.

This strategy, to their surprise, was effective. They had adhered to it for the past two and half years. And now Alma was about to sabotage it. She couldn't help it. She couldn't talk about this problem in the kitchen or the living room, upright, like an adult. She could only talk about this in their bed with his arms around her and her face in his chest, pretending she didn't half own this house and all its appliances, was just some runaway waif he'd taken in, out of the goodness of his heart, to comfort and shelter and feed.

"I shouldn't have talked to the parents first," she said. "I should have asked him first thing. Caught him off guard, so he couldn't make something up."

Kurt whispered, "Shouldn't we go into the bathroom or something?"

Alma laughed. Then she felt sad. This was the persona they had invented for their sex life. It was like a baby, but an ironic baby, a phantom baby, a baby whose dependence and touchiness were gently sneered at.

"The thing is," she said, "maybe he *can't* be caught off guard. You should see how he behaves. It makes me suspect ritualized Satanic abuse—you know, brainwashing and repro-gramming."

Kurt laughed. "Come on."

Alma lifted her head and stared at him.

"What if he's doing this to *himself*?"

Kurt's brow furrowed. "What, like self-mutilating?"

"Kids do that! If there's trauma, or even as a compulsive thing, to relieve anxiety. What if he's doing this and he's telling his parents it's from sports, and *they're* making up another story to explain it to themselves, and meanwhile all three of them are too ashamed to really talk about it? . . . Oh, fuck. I messed this up."

Kurt rubbed her back as she kept going. "It's not about me," she said. "It's not about my ego. It's not about my ego . . ." She could have gone on chanting this mantra, but already the initial shock and guilt were beginning to wear off.

"I am fucked," she said slowly.

Kurt shifted onto one elbow. "This is *all* speculation," he said. "All of it. It's time to hand it over to social services."

Alma was quiet, feeling his eyes on her.

"That feels so drastic," she said. "They could put him in a group home, traumatize him even more. It could ruin everyone's life."

Kurt rolled over on his back and stared at the bedroom ceiling.

"When *I* was eight," he said to the ceiling, "my life would've changed for the better if some professional authority had noticed what was going on, marched into the house, and said, in front of me, 'No, this is not acceptable, you don't hit your kid with a fireplace poker,' and taken me the fuck out of there."

He spoke as if he'd wanted to say this to her for a long time. Kurt hardly ever talked about his past. And he never swore.

"I'm just saying," he added, almost defiantly. Then he saw that Alma's eyes were full of tears.

He sat up. "You're a good person," he told her. "You love those kids."

Alma shook her head. She wanted to say more, but his dis-

closure had dwarfed every justification and shadowy feeling
she had, and she clammed up, abashed.

"I don't know," she said. "I don't know if I do."

It was 3:46 a.m. when she left the house. Kurt was asleep on
his stomach, one arm heavy and dangling over the edge of the
bed, and she dressed as quietly as she could. Outside, the lawn
sparkled with frost and all familiar landmarks looked mischie-
vous and unreliable. Alma could feel each tine of cilia in her
nose stiffen and separate as she turned the key in the ignition
and backed out.

She didn't stop to think about what she was doing because
that would have kept her from doing it. And she wasn't really
doing anything, anyway: she just wanted to see the house. The
school directory was on the passenger seat, opened to the G's
with the Grissom address circled in pen: 1195 Hightower
Road. She and Kurt passed it every winter en route to Hobbs'
Christmas Tree Farm.

She had some foggy but ironclad notion that if she saw the
house, stood in front of it and watched it in the dark, she
would be able to intuit whether there was anything truly bad
inside. Alma did not believe in auras or phantasms but she did
believe in impressions, in the homespun integrity of hunches,
and she also believed that the best way of confronting a mys-
tery was to bear dogged, mute witness: merely placing oneself
in front of the enigma like a ghostly apparition before a mur-
derer, looming over it in dumb reproach until it revealed its
secret. So she would go and stare at the house. What it came
down to was reliability of perspective: she trusted no eyes but
her own. She drove past the waterfront, its pier like a plank

into an abyss, the lighthouse rising out of the choppy foam of
Lake Superior, then crossed the railroad tracks and entered
what she thought of as the "real" Beulah: fields dotted with
scarecrow trees, rotting barns, and acres and acres of blueberry
farms edged in migrant shacks with torn T-shirts tacked to
their windows.

She knew that the unpaved side roads led to working farms,
snug and tight, and seventies-era ramblers on acres of wood-
lands, with in-ground pools and the occasional hot tub.
Hightower, a half mile past the Mr. Turkey processing plant,
was one of these roads: inhabited by people who stocked their
freezers with venison but also took day trips to the casinos in
Traverse City. She spotted 1195 before she was ready to, and
skidded to a stop on the pebbled shoulder.

Alma doused her lights and stepped out of the car. Then
she stood and stared at the house where Peter was presumably
sleeping, and where the mysterious thing that hurt him was
sleeping, too, harmless in its deactivated state but still there, a
daily part of that household: she could tell. And the house
itself—a tan-sided rancher, well maintained, with a new-
looking roof and spotless gutters and a glaring sodium spotlight carving out a triangle of brightness on the garage door's
silver-plated Roman numerals—was beside the point. It was a
nice house. Kurt, she remembered, had grown up in a nice
house, too.

Something rustled in the crackle-dry brush behind her, and
Alma jumped and turned in time to see a dark bulky mass lum-
bering past, low to the ground. From its air of furtive haste and
the tunneling determination of its progress, she knew it was a
wild animal. And there in the dark between Peter's house and

the woods, she thought of the raccoon story. The one-year-old girl had screamed during the attack, and her parents *must* have heard her screaming; the pole barn was too small for them to sleep through it. But they didn't get up. They let her scream. The next morning they rose and saw the raccoon crouched in a corner with blood on its muzzle. Only then did they lean over the crib and look at the child, who was no longer screaming.

Alma had puzzled over this. She tried to put herself in the place of the couple: exhausted, no longer in love, at their wits' end, loath to get up and tend a screeching baby they never wanted in the first place, a baby whose conception must have felt like a nasty trick dooming them to Beulah and the pole barn and each other for eternity. How numb did they have to be in order to fail to discern a cry of mortal terror from one of idle plaint? But the worst was when Alma stopped speculating on parental motives and began to inhabit, slowly and by degrees, the child's agony, that ink-black well of wordless victimhood where logic and behavioral psychology lost all meaning. It was a collective nightmare of the unconscious, everyone's worst dream: to be steeped in great danger and unable to articulate it, to run or fight or tell. As for the child, who lived, Alma was certain that if she remembered anything at all it would be not the attack but the screaming, and lying there waiting to be found.

A tiger, Peter had said. Another bogeyman of the unconscious: primal and immune to reason. All of a sudden his outlandish excuse—which had seemed to her merely flippant, cynical, like signing *Luke Skywalker* on the attendance sheet—seemed poignant for a boy so little given to fantasy and invention. What if the big cat was wish fulfillment, a prowling protector like something out of C. S. Lewis? Alma thought of the baby in its crib, of Kurt in primary school with a broken tailbone, hiding it. How he never sat with his back to an empty room. The world seemed at that moment brimming with damage and the encoded responses to it, everyone around her wearing it on their sleeve, not just Peter and Kurt and the baby but their parents and grandparents and all the animals and trees and vacant lots and sprawling, hopefully built houses, the very woods behind her swaying with grief.

Alma got back in her car. It was still dark. When she pulled into her driveway she saw Kurt bundled in his parka on the front porch, with the spotlight on, waiting for her.

They had a talk. If she didn't call social services, Kurt said, he would.

"Going over there like a vigilante in the middle of the night is not going to do any good," he said. "You are not trained to handle this."

They sat in the kitchen. Alma looked over her coffee mug at the window, the gray and pink sky.

"It's dangerous," Kurt said.

Alma snapped at him. "Do you know how bad it would make me look if *you* called social services? Give me a few days to try and figure out what the hell is going on here. Then I'll talk to the school counselor. And *she'll* be the one to call. That's how it's *done*."

Kurt stared at her with a complete lack of recognition. It frightened her. She didn't know how to make him understand that her reluctance to involve the authorities wasn't a denial of

Peter's personhood but an affirmation of it, of his prickly exasperating individuality and the endless extenuating circumstances it implied. By calling the authorities she would consign Peter to one-dimensionality, flattened and filed. She was not ready to do that.

Kurt turned away from her and looked into the sink. His hair stuck up at crazy angles and she wanted nothing more than to smooth it down and hug his body to her like a giant hot water bottle, but she was afraid he would rebuff her. Their arguments always brought her to the same dead end. The dark places in Alma's own background were insufficient to trump the fact that she had not been beaten. It was like an endless, rigged game of Rock Paper Scissors. Beating crushed everything.

Kurt's back was still turned. "Three days," he said stiffly. "Can we say three days?"

"Okay," Alma said. "Fine."

On the first day, Peter had no new wounds. When she handed him the lavatory pass, he gave her a close-lipped, reflexive smile and a dip of the head, like someone accepting a proffered seat on a crowded bus.

"Peter," she said. She spoke low, so he had to lean in to hear her. "I'd like your parents to come in after school tomorrow for a chat. Will you tell them?"

"Okay," he said.

But he was absent the next day. Alma, calling roll, stood silent in front of the class a beat too long when she didn't get an answer. During recess she went to the administrative office.

"Grissom," the secretary repeated, scanning her triplicate three-ring message log. She tore out a pink slip of paper. "Yes," she said. "His mother called it in."

On the slip was written, in the secretary's bubbly cursive, *Son down with flu. Can't make meeting tonight. Reschedule?*

Alma thanked the secretary and put the note in her blazer pocket. Then she walked to the faculty bathroom and locked herself in a stall. "Shit," she hissed. It was supposed to be over tonight. She was supposed to sleep well, her decision made; she was supposed to go home and tell Kurt, *I got to the bottom of it* or *I'm telling the counselor tomorrow.*

But it wasn't over, and she imagined Peter—who had shown no signs of flu the day before—was now so severely disfigured that his parents had to hide him until he healed. Or until she forgot. But she wouldn't forget.

Alma left the bathroom and banged her way through the lounge, where she found the kindergarten teacher, Mrs. Crayborn, preparing to leave after a half-day of alphabet songs and picture books. "Lily," she panted, "I have an emergency." She felt a brief, crazed surge of resentment for the older woman, whose students were too young to resort to subterfuge.

Mrs. Crayborn agreed to sub for her. As soon as she got the go-ahead Alma was out the door and running, slipping on the frosty asphalt toward her car, jamming the key in, on her way to Hightower Road to end Peter Grissom's suffering. And yet, as she drove, she felt that he was expecting her, summoning her, not as a victim awaiting rescue but as a cornered criminal orchestrating a grandly self-destructive finale as the prelude to surrender.

But that's ridiculous, Alma told herself as she parked in the

Grissoms' driveway. The tan ranch-style house blinked in the bright sun, like something innocent and just wakened. She hadn't abandoned her class and driven to the middle of nowhere in order to outsmart an eight-year-old. She was not here to satisfy her own ego. She was here because Kurt was right, after all. She loved her students, all of them, even the ones she didn't like. They broke her heart. Not because their lives were bad, but because she saw their personalities forming day to day and some of them had such charisma, such wily quirky charm, and others were so shy and kind, and once in a while she'd fleetingly recognize some familiar, adaptive, adultlike tic in their facial expressions or voices—the way they'd leap into a conversation to say their piece or brusquely brush off an advance would remind her of her favorite aunt, say, or her old boyfriend from college. And it was somehow sad to see such identifiable traits in such miniature packages, like baby animals whose paws were far too big for their bodies. The traits were so much more endearing in people who didn't know how to wield them. Each child was a particular type of person—the type to bring a book on a plane to ward off garrulous strangers, the type to *be* a garrulous stranger—and they didn't know it yet. But saddest of all were the ones who *did* know, and too soon, the ones like Peter—measured and mindful and autonomous, as if he'd gotten his hands on some manual of socialization too advanced for his age, as if he'd been, crime of crimes, *reading ahead*, while continuing to sing the old songs and play the old games so as not to hurt her feelings. He was already the person he would become.

When he opened the door in response to her ring, wearing Batman pajamas and old moccasins, too big, that must have been his father's, it seemed incredible to Alma that he could materialize so readily at her behest. He held a box of Kleenex under one arm.

"What's going on?" he said. His voice was thick with phlegm.

"Peter," Alma said, "where are your parents?"

He wiped his nose with one sleeve. "At work."

"Both of them?"

"Yeah."

"So who's taking care of you?"

"I'm not that sick," he said scornfully, wearily. But clearly he was sick: red encrusted nostrils, gummed-up voice, the shaky, wrung-out posture of the feverish. Other than that, there appeared to be nothing wrong with him. Alma heard a TV in the background.

"Peter," she said, "you need to let me in the house."

For a second Peter, in his weakened state, seemed to be auditioning various excuses in his head. But he stepped aside and let Alma into the foyer. Then he shuffled ahead of her, toward the sound of the TV, and disappeared.

Alma looked around. The foyer was neat, if rather barren and neutral in an artless way. The floors were cream tile, the beige walls hung with the occasional family photo: Peter's school picture, his golden face washed out by harsh lighting, smiling with tolerant forbearance against the marbled blue background; and a studio portrait of Peter flanked by his kneeling parents, all smiling with great restraint, as if to temper the folksy excess of the fake farm-scene backdrop.

The kitchen was beige as well, with white tile counters and sage-green stenciling of a leaf pattern around the crown mold-ing. In the sink Alma found two coffee-stained ceramic mugs and a plastic Pokémon bowl dusted with the remains of cereal. She opened the fridge, took a liter of 7-Up from the side shelf, and poured a glassful: the treat her mother used to give her when she had the flu. She thought of Popsicles, but in the freezer she found only an empty ice tray and stacks of thick, frost-furred red meat, one on top of the other.

She followed the drone of the TV into the living room, where Peter was lying on a brown corduroy sectional sofa in front of *Wheel of Fortune*. When Alma handed him the glass he took it with his polite, tucked-in little smile/nod, and downed half in a single gulp.

"Did anyone take your temperature?" Alma said.

Peter rubbed his forehead. "It's way down from last night," he rasped.

They sat and stared at the TV. Alma kept looking around for some revealing object. But the only item in the room that stood out to her was a pink ceramic horse on a carousel pole, still in its packaging, clearly a gift, gingerly placed on its side on the coffee table.

"Peter," Alma said, "I'm going to stay here until your parents get home from work. Then all three of us are going to have a talk."

"It's hard for me to talk right now," he croaked, tapping his throat with one finger.

"I know. But I need to know what's happening." Peter reached for the glass again, his pajama sleeve riding up, and that was when she saw it: a small, fresh gouge on his forearm, encircled with dried blood. More stripes overlaid the wound, vertical and bright red. They were embossed in fierce relief.

Before he could pull his sleeve down Alma pounced and grabbed his wrist, felt it warm and startled in her grasp—sinewy, like an animal, with an animal's refusal to relax into her touch—and said, "I need to know what's going on with *this*."

Peter extricated his wrist. Then he said, "I already told you."

Alma could have bowed her head and laughed, or cried. How sick she was of this boy: his cryptic utterances, his ridiculous changeling shtick. How sick she was of all of them. Of the repetitions, the rhyming and chanting, the careful planting of subliminal associations, the brick-by-brick banking of remedial skills that would, if she did her job right, eventually be as effortless to them as breathing, so effortless as to negate their memory of her entirely. She was sick of dressing for them, lying awake for them, planning for them, shaping their twenty-three fragile brains in her hands, trying to reverse the damage already incurred, and failing as they all watched her. In fact, she had never felt more watched in her life as she did right then, sitting on the couch next to Peter. But it wasn't the old feeling of being spied on by twenty-three children. This feeling was altogether different: reptilian and chilling, a sensation of being watched keenly, flatly, with one-dimensional singularity of purpose. And not by Peter. He wasn't watching her at all. He was suddenly looking past her toward the narrow hallway that led to the bedrooms. His wan face slowly flushed, softened, rearranged itself in a gently morphing way that reminded Alma of when her nephew was born, how his head changed shape as it emerged from the birth canal.

Afterward, Alma would say that she knew what it was before

she even turned around. That she knew, with a certainty so age-old it felt primitive, that it could only be one thing. And on some level this was true. But it also wasn't. All she knew, in the split second before she turned her head, was that there was something behind her that did not belong there. She sensed a juxtaposition so audacious and profoundly wrong that it created a ruptured seam at the place of intersection. Beyond that she had no image in mind, least of all the one she, following Peter's gaze, finally beheld: a tiger cub, motionless, sitting on the demarcation between living room and hallway.

The cub was more than half the length of Peter. Alma couldn't tell if it was changing position or if she was imagining it. The air around it shimmered queasily, like a hologram. Then it really did begin to move, stalking slowly and without sound, and Alma, frozen on the couch, watched it come closer: its stiff white whiskers, rigid as quills, the satiny, blockish mitts of its paws, the polar ruff around its face and the spine snaking across its back, painterly black stripes on either side, and finally the fiery liquor of its small eyes, black-rimmed, staring into hers.

What she saw there was neither menace nor bloodlust but something worse: the hard glaze of majestic incomprehension. And everything else about the tiger's posture—the twitching tail, compressed muscularity, the jutting dorsal fins of its perfect shoulder blades—told her she was committing an unforgivable trespass, that she had unknowingly bumbled into the terrible and debased presence of God, gone to seed.

Peter tumbled off the sofa, hurled himself at the tiger, and threw his arms around its neck.

"Peter," Alma snapped. "Get back over here!" She half

stood, but something about the scene made her waver in mid-stance and sink back down again: Peter was not listening to her. He was covering the tiger's neck with kisses. He crooned into its ear. His hands roved over its stripes, avid, shaky. His eyes were closed. And the tiger bore these caresses with royal indifference, occasionally jawing lightly at Peter's neck or face. It yawned, and she saw the row of gleaming top teeth and the flat, silver-barbed tongue.

There was something mythically foreboding about the scene that paralyzed Alma—intimations of Mowgli, Romulus and Remus, this besotted child basking in the imperially fierce bounty of a predator who, by not killing him, was committing a noble act of dispensation. She forced herself to stand up.

Peter was crying.

"I told you," he said. "I told you the truth and you said I wouldn't get in trouble."

"You won't," Alma said. "Step away from that thing. Slowly."

"Don't tell anyone," he said. "If you do they'll take him away. My dad said so. He's not hurting anyone. He's just a baby."

"Peter," she said. "Please. Please, honey. Get up and come toward me."

Tears streamed down his face and dappled the fur of the tiger cub. It shook its head irritably at the sensation.

"Peter," she said, "I'm just going to walk over there and pet the tiger. Okay? I just want to pet him. That's all I'm going to do." She raised her hands palms-up.

To her surprise and grief, Peter bought it. He nodded, eyes still wary but tentatively open to trust, and as he wiped his nose on his sleeve and waited for her to approach, Alma felt like an unwilling bride, ceremonial and slow, advancing toward a fate she had not chosen. And she felt that the least she could do was touch the animal, that she owed Peter that, and when she was close enough she extended her hand. She smelled Peter—an earthy smell cut through with eucalyptus rub—and, closing her eyes, she sensed his warm eagerness. *Pretend it's a stuffed animal,* she told herself. But she felt the tiger's bristling life before she even touched it, the instinctive outrage coded deep, and then her fingertips grazed a fuzzy aureole—an ear, she guessed—that jerked with swift, brute integrity at her touch. Her eyes opened.

She grabbed Peter around the waist and heaved him up, staggering to her feet, crossing the room with him thrashing and crying and hanging from her arms, and they made tortur-ous progress toward the kitchen, where there was a phone—all Alma could think of was, *The phone, the phone,* like it was the neutral territory in a game of tag—and before the kitchen door slammed behind them she saw the tiger, sitting up, stern and unreadable, as if watching the graceless retreat of maimed prey not worth chasing.

For the rest of Alma's life, whenever she told this story, people would ask her what went through her mind. They meant at the moment she saw the tiger. The rest—the call to 911, the dragging of Peter into his bedroom so he wouldn't see the tranquilizing dart going in and the limp striped body carried out, her refusal to talk to the local paper for its exposé on illegal exotic animal breeding—was easy to understand. But they all wanted to know what she felt at the exact second she saw the tiger, and their eagerness was greedy and sheepish, like they were about to receive information they knew was too sacred and complex to process, as though she'd had a near-death experience and was expected to tell them who or what she saw, bathed in light, at the end of the tunnel.

Alma had a stock answer. She felt terror, she would tell them, dutifully and more or less truthfully. Terror for the boy's safety and for her own. But in those first few seconds, she had not been afraid. She had felt a dark drumbeat of uneasy commiseration. Not between her and Peter, but between her and the tiger. This was what she could never tell anyone: that her first thought hadn't been, *Grab the boy,* or *Danger, danger.* What it had been, instead, was a question. As if in direct address to an old nemesis she had only ever encountered in shadow, she had looked into the tiger's face in broad daylight and thought, aghast, *What are you doing here?*

Neither would she tell anyone what passed between her and Peter in the kitchen, before she dialed the number. How she turned to him and said, "I'm sorry," really meaning it, and he just shook his head. She sensed his composure settling down around him again. She heard it in his voice, strangled as it was with phlegm and tears.

"No, you're not," he told her. "But someday you will be."